This story is a work of fiction. Names, charac[ters]
imagined or are used [fictitiously.]

Copyright © 2014 by Phil Saroyan

All rights reserved.

ISBN 978-1-4675-5816-7

Old Harbor Delight

A moist marine layer formed outside in the middle of the day, a day after what was yet another fabulous day in Old Harbor. The fog was a welcome reprieve to what would normally be dry, stark heat.

As a beach city, Old Harbor was well-known for being a magnate for the 'ultra' crowd, attracting ethereal beauty and glamor. People were revered here. This was a place.

A strong community existed here that normally only existed for the small, upper-crust neighborhoods and boroughs, Old Harbor possessed a rare combination of sensibility and hysteria. Anyone who was anyone was known here, everyone else was an outsider. Yet there was a certain congeniality bequeathed on those who were débutantes, dilettantes and onlooking sophomores.

Party crowds came by the droves, and even those who would normally have hard liquor and drugs found themselves rudimentary and un-trendy here.

Mixology was a certain vogue. Drinking: a fashion statement, and a way of life for the youth here. Vodka, cranberry, gin and tonic, beer, sparkling cider; they were all simple precursors. But people didn't visit Old Harbor for just any drink, they came for a signature drink known as 'Old Harbor Delight'.

It was special, often made for bright young faces, and even for older folks who had known better than to walk into any old rum shack unless it was for a righteous imbibing.

People here frequently picnicked with their merlots, and new-fangled cheeses, accompanied by friends, colleagues, and lovers. An active art culture kept the city rich with desire; it was a wine lover's paradise, certain titles rivaled even that of France's Bordeaux. The art and wine went hand-in-hand; eventually attracting more and more diverse peoples, and greater business.

A colony of young entrepreneurs, aficionados, wild artists, actors, filmmakers, old money and trust fund babies led the way in the budding years of Old Harbor's successful wine trade. Each year the city grew richer, thanks to the wine auctions bidding higher for Zinfandels, Merlots, Pinot Noirs—and Champagne—the pinnacle of their success.

The grapes were all grown in the fields of Old Harbor and some adjacent regions. The heat of the nearby regions was too dry, but the beaches made temperatures cool enough to make good tasting wine grapes. The morning dew, the marine layer, and the sea breeze cultivated a grape that was soft-tasting for its age. The sparkling wine it produced had a very distinct, palatable flavor, even to those who scrunched their faces at the mere thought of wine. It somehow made a statement. Sparkling, crystallized, soft from the soil; soft from the sea breeze, it seemed to glitter in people's mouths. People spoke of it as though it were glitter, as though they were children who could speak of it as such. Yet, it was also savory as much as it was sweet. It fizzed around the top of the mouth as good pop should, and went down with no aftertaste, an equal balance of sweet and savory. Connoisseurs coined its flavor 'ocean butter'. The originators christened the champagne in token of its light flavor and bright effects on the mind. This champagne produced a bona-fide therapeutic effect with studies showing this grade of pop could soothe mild depression and restlessness. That was, of course, a very well calculated advertisement.

'Old Harbor Lights', as it was called, was served on ice. Other versions, less prized, were mixed with pale ales. Mixing the two produced a velvet finish. It was the drink most requested by those better accustomed to Old Harbor. They consumed it spritely, cerebrally, experiencing what sight itself could only guess. It was as consistent as champagne, but was more of a nectar, produced by the fruit of the soil. The least part of the drink was champagne, the rest was ale. It couldn't have been any more a nectar with most parts champagne; and, all parts champagne didn't make it a signature drink at all. Its sight and chemistry was also appreciated with a vicissitude that gave it a distinct texture.

This drink made people giddy in its consumption. Far different than simple martinis or ordinary pop, it was an elixir of sorts; and for many, it had a crescendo to its effects. Though, it also made people dangerously intoxicated.

Nothing was impossible having a glass of this wine. On the coast, life was like a dream, the waves' crests mimicked the bobbing froth. A brisk, creamy victory of whitewash in each pour. Aged in the oak barrels of Old Harbor, it fast became

3

recognized as one of the world's greatest, spurring brands, images and labels to follow, eventually producing the same buzz of an ethereal high society. It symbolized the spoils of success, extravagant lifestyles, and smitten games, all leading to a violent endgame and fight for power.

Egalitarian at one time, Old Harbor was made rich by its grape vineyards, manned by so-called descendants of France. Considering its success, the wine trade was cause for envy and corruption. It would eventually confront social clashes and contempt for those who held the reins to the city's trade. Before its immense success, Old Harbor's fields were enriched by the stable hands and mighty souls who had bared witness to many fables. But this was a new chapter, one marked by lust, greed and contempt, feigned by great pretenses.

A hot spring day in Old Harbor, two young things who had reached the age of majority, met under the same blue sky, and were destined by one force or another. A Leo and a Scorpio. A famed, young debutant—Philipe Bollinger—had polite good looks, was charming and of a respectable intellectual capacity. Therefore, it was no surprise that he would have to fight his desire every time he laid eyes on Sally, a fine young doe, and, yet a heartbreaker, she had been going out with the infamous bruiser, Rainor, son of the revered sept clan.

Sally rode horses in the springtime. She grew up with horses, and trained them in the pre-season, that's where she met Philipe for the first time. He had seemed completely laconic to her, he never dared exchange a single word, but he had boyish charm and the intelligent looks that she liked.

Her boyfriend Rainor, came to visit her, however, abruptly, at the paddock. His appearance was odd to her because he rarely made a trip like this, this late in the afternoon. Of course, she was thrilled to see him, at any rate, so her emotions got the better of her. Their intimacy in the paddock was very awkward to Philipe, who couldn't help but wonder what was going on between them, sensing that Sally was becoming upset, by the sound of her conversation with Rainor. After about twenty minutes, Rainor left the paddock, and Sally was helplessly crying in tears.

As Rainor crossed paths with Philipe, a tinge of a dark-grey complexion came out of him next to Philipe and his shiny white horse. They locked eyes for a second with a look that could carve stone.

4

Philipe found Sally huddled up inside the paddock; searching into her shiny, teary eyes, he offered her solace. He was always warm to her, although never saying much, he was familiar enough to her. He reminded her of this warmth as he tried to console her weeping heart.

"What's the matter?" He asked. "What's going on?"

"Rainor says I'm pushing him aside too much, he says I'm not there for him..." She wept incredulous to her own speech. "He's dumping me..." A waterfall of tears began to pour out of her, the weight of the break-up became too much for her. "I gave him everything a man could want." Still teary-eyed, she forcefully attempted to pout less hard, to keep her composure. "What does he give me?" She said emotionally. "He dumps me. He doesn't write me love letters; he doesn't share anything in his life with me. So why he is so appalled that I want and need so much?" She surrendered into Philipe's arms, squeezing him tightly.

"I'm not pushing him away, I have work and been busy training 'Lucky' here, and busy with school; and a million other things to worry about, just as he does..."

"Have you talked to him about this before?" Philipe prodded.

Looking at him for a second, she relinquished. This might have been the biggest exchange of words they ever had with each other. "You feel so good to me Philipe..." Changing her tone of voice, "Why haven't you ever tried talking to me?" She asked. "I know you like me."

"You do? ...I mean what makes you say that?"

"The way you look at me, you don't take your eyes off me. When I'm with 'Lucky', in the paddock, I see you, your eyes burn right through me."

"I've hardly ever said more than a 'hello' to you..."

"Hold me tighter Philipe. I'm cold."

The two cuddled closer to each other, near enough to hear their two hearts beating. A moment of warmth and relief faded into becoming a moment of awkward silence.

"So how has 'Lucky' been doing?" Philipe finally asked.

5

"Oh, she's been fabulous. I'm out here more and more each season. It wouldn't surprise me if she goes on to win first place in her next competition, even though she's moving up in class. How about your horse? I imagine she's been doing very well."

"She's been a winning horse so far." Philipe replied, "Still haven't pushed her to the limit yet... You're welcome to come with me, this weekend's her next race..."

Sally looked at him with a cheer. "Ya? I would go with you, like as your girlfriend?" Philipe did not object. "I would love that." She said.

"Are you single?" She asked.

"I have a long-distance relationship." He replied. "Mainly on the phone... I write her frequently." He said in his defense.

"Oh ya? Like letters, you write her letters?"

"On occasion, why?" He said, still on his defensive.

"No reason... do you write her love letters?"

"Yes. I do." He said firmly.

Sally clasped tighter onto him, she was completely in his arms now. Worked up emotionally and physically, Philipe smacked her on the lips with a kiss that lasted longer than a normal kiss, leaving their lips pout. It was the only warmth in the frigid, cold paddock, and their first display of public affection. Their hearts were pounding.

Deceit and corruption lurked around the corner in Old Harbor, it was far from being one city, it was perfectly divided into two parts: uptown and downtown. Downtown was the business center and nervous system; uptown was a quintessential art district. The wine trade was a unifier in what would otherwise be a constant battle between both sides.

Appreciation for the arts, and cultivation of the grape, was not part of the endgame here. In the same way that youth find what they are looking for without seeking, so did Old Harbor's youth, consumed by cultism.

Perhaps the older generations would have appealed, somehow, if they knew what was taking place. Like the musketeer to a young knight unknowing of a sword or a scepter, no less from his foes', the youth did not know the dangerous liaisons and follies of corruption that were neatly covered up. This was a group of young people cultivated to act like a sect, and a cult. In exchange, they were given enough autonomy to live by their own rules in the underground. Their leaders were hapless souls, all too familiar with the dregs of society; dangerous people who wildly craved money and fame, and willing to obtain it at all costs. As inglorious as they were, their place within mainstream society had already been formed. And like any come-uppance, they would have to make sacrifices.

As though prophesizing, artists depicted unruly social clashes in their works; such as an adaptation of the "Lord of The Flies" painting, and other works resigned to fiction in pop culture. They were becoming overwhelmingly contemptuous towards the rich, yet kept their true feelings suppressed and short. They were hardly innocent, however, with Old Harbor's underground riddled by apocrypha. Yet, all their hatred was in of itself imbued by the very people they were opposed, the rich families and heads of estates.

Not undone by their own quest for power and riches, the underground youth were as ambitious as young Turks with a simple agenda: multiply wealth and recruit en masse. Uncanny in their habits of spending money; they shared a proclivity for symbolism, to make them iconic. Rights and exclusivity were given to members who paid in; friends of equal wealth and status could become rank members as so-called shared blood in the interest of multiplying. Those highest on the totem pole were sure to brandish young blood by recognizing only familiar regalia and violently keeping their underlings in check. Outsiders would tattoo their bodies in a similar fashion to resemble a familiar crest, but were seldom accepted and recognized, yet their allegiance to the underground movement grew stronger.

Many artists knew of local cults through family and friends. And with their secrets growing more and more fabled, artists kept their myths encoded in paintings and movies, still underground from the mainstream. People often spoke in maths that touched upon current affairs, not to be spoken of directly. It was a revelation that could be manufactured, a rabbit hole of sorts, and it was recounting a moral story far more dangerous than its previous fables. Many feared the underground would eventually take over the city like locusts.

Downtown, being as were, a far cry from a city metropolis, was still where people made their money in the wine trade and various other exports. It smelled like the Old Harbor countryside, with pellets and crates full of herbs, fruits and various wine barrels. All of it going through the main artery of trade off the nearby coast. The northern entrance to town famously waved a French flag on so-called Annulet St.

A Franco-American legion held the reins to most of the wine estates in the region, comprised of few families, including the Bollinger's, the Petit's and the LeBlanc's, benefactors of old French tradition. Steeped in austerity, somehow, they escaped modernity in Old Harbor, all to the bane of the working class who toiled for modest wages. It wasn't that the working class felt oppressed by them, but it made them bitter, and was cause of much envy and spite towards the rich. There was no reason in the minds of the working individuals and families, why they shouldn't have the same exploits and indulgences as their stodgy counterparts. After all, the rich estate owners did nothing for the betterment of everyday society, other than to further their own ends. And they were very haughty in embellishing their possessions and dwellings, which were hardly lived in, or so they thought...

The heads of the wine estates had their own family coat of arms, sharing the insignia of old monarchs. It was a color-coated fleur-de-lys', which seemed ridiculous, how this amount of importance and austerity could still exist in such things...

Yet, it was so, anachronistic from the outside, dead-serious on the inside. They argued that by their lobbying and politicking, they had enriched society in the area, bringing wealth, no matter if it was only for the sake of the wine trade. The land, although rich in soil, was entirely worthless, before the cultivation of grape vineyards. They drove a hard bargain as well, bidding the prices up for their local wine and champagne, unheard of before in Old Harbor. Taking all the credit for the so-called 'Old Harbor Lights', it became the top champagne, and choice drink, thanks to some clever marketing.

Uptown was wildly different than downtown, more focused on art, and contemptuous towards business. It was full of boutique artists, mainly rustic painters and jewelers. Annulet Street embodied the art and prestige.

Passing through the heart of downtown and uptown was a river jetty that neatly divided the two parts of Old Harbor. Uptown was the northern entry into the city with a stately mansion, known as the Annulet Chateau, serving as a bed and breakfast to greet visitors. It was the first thing people saw when entering. It was also a historic landmark with a black and silver fleur-de-lys embossed on the ground of its

8

entrance, inscribed with names of all its previous owners, one including the Bollinger family name. A narrow street—Annulet St.— led into the old estate, and now served as a bed and breakfast. It was so narrow that a normal flow of traffic could not pass through it. Shrouded in lavender and bougainvillea, it was a pedestrian promenade with cottage-like boutiques and one of the city's most outrageous anachronisms, Candy's Cantina. The cantina was a decrepit rum shack that had the foul smell of vomit and urine.

Most locals did not cross over from uptown to downtown much. The conflict between the two was palpable, and was not so much a tourist attraction. Just as well, commercial prosperity did not spill over from downtown to uptown. Uptown was less desirable commercially, as it also suffered from occasional bouts of fights and burglaries. Yet, it still managed to attract people serious about their art, despite it being the stomping grounds for a budding cult. If it weren't for the crime and notoriety surrounding it, uptown wouldn't have been seen so blighted in the eyes of the quaint, decent people of Old Harbor, because they were somewhat protected by these fight rousers.

The highest of them inspired a deep-rooted clansman mentality, tied with the departed 'septs', only a few were actually related with the so-called sept clans, while many others claimed to be one, but were merely a front. This was yet another cause for conflict in Old Harbor's underground.

Surfacing rumors, some had said that certain members of the 'sept' clans existed within the police force, but the distinction was not made entirely clear, a constant impetus for checks and balances from within. It was very hard to make the distinction between the legitimate and the dilettantes, much less were the French able to differentiate the two out of sheer ignorance, or apathy. This confluence of cult and clan was Byzantine to the French, they had pronounced it "riddled", just as their process of making champagne. They needed them, but as far as they were concerned, they were better off without them.

Most people commonly thought they were part of the sept, but it only consisted of six family surnames. Traditionally, that meant there would be six family crests, but the six families had banded together in previous times, as was common in their history. This understanding gave members a fight to become top rank from within their multiple recruits. The highest ones wore a ring on their left hand, an heirloom passed down by their fathers and forefathers. Their crest symbol was the head of two lions and a sword. In tradition, this was an invalid crest symbol, but was

9

supported by modern convention, without any false pretenses or concerns of being scrutinized by royal purveyors, and such. People believed it was true, so it was accepted. The tiny glitch existing in their clan's identity was a story of alliances, won and lost. The cult and its members shamelessly wore their own version of the coat of arms with the lion's emblem on their chests to imitate true members of the sept, thinking it was of equal logic to their counterparts' coat of arms. Yet, cult members were mere subjects and lesser mortals, without any veracity for staking a claim of equal import to the sept. They were mere representations.

The emblem worn by the sept was nearly identical to the traditional crest of the Royal Army of Scotland. This cadency was also co-opted by the illegitimate cult. In addition, the sept members were required to have a tattoo of the cross Moline on their arm. They were seen as a protective clan, and some in the police force did have cadency to the sept. But, the illegitimate members in the underground were numerous among them. Instead of protecting the city, many rogue members ran afoul, in a quest towards their own selfish ends, even fanning out a self-proclaimed aristocracy, borne out of corruption. The more one tried to fight against this perceived torrent, the more they learned how corrupt it was.

Rainor, son of Gregor, was of Roman Catholic and Scottish descent, a poster child of clan legacy, and of modest means. He was a down-to-earth, good guy, for the most part, but not one to cross given his rank in the patriarchy. He hated living up to his expectations, but he had to when he was in the public eye.

So when the Bollinger estate was hosting a debutante party, he was hesitant to attend, and although Rainor wasn't exactly a social butterfly, he wouldn't turn down an invitation of this import.

At the party, he was hard to miss. Far from being animated, he was entertaining yet, he had a very impressive demeanor and upright posture, and commanded presence. Although Rainor didn't care so much what people thought of him, he was at his most vulnerable at a party like this. Among his peers were plenty of sycophant artists and wanna-be clansmen, all with a vicious intent on getting more of a piece of him and the likeness of him. Certainly, no one envisioned that these wannabes had ulterior motives.

Early in the night, searchlights lit up Uptown for a movie premiere. There was food and wine and red carpet for local society and celebrities, including Keith—

Rainor's blood cousin. Keith's true name was Philipe, but had changed it to distance himself from the Gregor family, who had written him off as a circus freak. He was the black sheep, with an upbringing that was far removed from the normal gentrification of the Gregor life. Keith was a drinker, a gambler, and a womanizer, the whole package deal of a loveable heathen, an animal, really. He dressed like one too; he looked like a wild leopard at the event.

Keith had an aunt, Katherine, who he was close to as an infant. She was the one who loved him the most as a child, but she became very prone to illness. She would become sickly most of the year in Old Harbor from the relentless Indian summers that lingered. She took vacations to Ireland, which eased her stress from the constant sunlight. She loved it so much, she decided she would make a new life for herself there with a new family. It had made her distant from life in Old Harbor. She was somewhat estranged from her family and society, nobody visited her in Ireland, since she lived in remote backcountry. Her only connections were phone calls to her widowed sister and some postcards to family and friends in Ireland.

The movie premiere attracted people from all over, as it was also time of wine harvest, this brought the bulk of tourism in the area.

Keith and his girlfriend, Karma, shared a limousine with their dear friends, Faith and her boyfriend, Grey, who were all very much the party-going type. All were completely made up with big make-up, jewelry, fancy clothes, fake tans and all. This was one of the annual parties that glorified their society and small town.

As an aspiring actor, Keith was staying in the limelight for all his latest projects. Arriving in style, and fashionably late, the four of them jostled to the red carpet, already buzzed from drinking from the limo.

Photographers gravitated to Keith and his friends as they jumped out of the limo. Talking to the cameras, it was all about his latest movie role: his character was a small-town hero living in a post-apocalyptic future in the movie they were premiering that night. He spoke for the longest out of everyone there, gleaning the rolling cameras, awaiting his moment to light up the red carpet.

He was dressed in a very snappy suit and fedora, wearing blue, leopard-skin, platform shoes, which made him an extra inch-and-a-half taller. Bulbs flashed in a frenzy of pictures as soon as he touched on. After what seemed like a full couple minutes of owning the red carpet, the rest of his entourage shared the moment with him as he embraced Faith's boyfriend for more pictures.

11

In the crowd of spectators, a drowned-out voice cried his birth name, "Philipe, Philipe! Oh, Philipe, over here, sweetheart! Over here!" Keith barely could hear, not even budging at the sound of her voice in the crowd. He didn't notice it was his aunt's voice, not one bit. And, he was trained by his agent not to respond to his christened name. Now that he was in the fame game, he responded to Keith, and only Keith. He was now getting paid to be the poster child of Old Harbor's clan culture. Philipe was just a small-town kid from a past life.

Sons of the patriarchs were assumed to be great consumers of alcohol, storytellers and hot-blooded fighters. Although Keith embodied that bad-boy image, he was really none of those things. As an actor, he was a one-trick pony and a typecast, his artistic talents were limited to that of a day-time actor. He managed to make a run for it doing full-features for lesser known names to make the scene.

Like all other actors, he would have been willing to take his next far-reaching role to elevate his career, but he was stuck, type-casted in the same underpaid roles. This movie was a slight victory for him with an evocative supporting role. Reviews and critics of the movie, 'Downtown Exile', raved on how bright Keith's future was with this role. He had to work for this gig by playing the fame game, which he was damn good at, that was his shtick, but like every other bit of fame, this would cost him. Tonight would be no exception.

With every vain pose and smirk, he was softly breaking his aunt's heart, the one person who loved him. She could only watch from a distance. From beginning to end, her nephew's vanity fair and seeming ignorance made her very emotional.

She was once a movie star dancer with all the connections in the world. She knew showbiz inside and out. And now she could only watch this peacock show, she didn't know whether to cry tears of joy or sorrow. All the reminders of her own desperate state, the rise and fall of fame... for a moment she was taken. It was surreal. Yet it was sad, incredibly sad.

She stood there, like her feet were stuck in cement. This world was revolving around her nephew, and she could see every folly and every turn of the corner of her nephew's imminent future. A sizable media outlet had their cameras in front of Keith, a news reporter fired off questions.

"So, Keith, tell us, and be honest, is your supporting role for 'Downtown Exile' based on the actual Rainor Gregor?" Keith let out a hearty laugh, hearing this, he replied, "Ya, you know, I think there's a little bit of Rainor in everyone, so,

12

really… it's based on all of the people people of Downtown." Stupefied, the anchor replied, "Oh?" "Yes, well it's true, isn't it?" Keith snapped back. "I mean look, I'm not trying to impersonate anyone. I would never hear the end of it. Besides, I flatter him enough already as it is." He glanced over at his entourage— "You saw the movie… what did you think of it?" "Very good, thank you very much Keith, and good luck." Keith simply shrugged in acquiescence, still managing to wink and turn a profile for every camera at the red carpet in a split second. He was moving, the cameras were chasing.

As the procession swept on to the movie premiere, those meeting Keith for the first time weren't going to forget him anytime soon, with all the face time and red-carpet hoopla.

Inside the theater, Keith's aunt was there among the captive audience, there was a moment of introspection, in the dark theater, she wondered if he remembered her at all, if he would recognize her when he saw her. She didn't feel sad though; she was content with what appeared to be modest success on her nephew's part being lauded as a local celebrity.

An hour-and-a-half later, the hoopla turned into drawn out beats and a glorified soap opera. The screening of the movie, although a glitzy production, dwindled down to its pathetic end, tragically leaving the audience in need of comic relief. Each scene poured over from one static image after another, a drowning of props and made-up actors without any real resolution or quest to fight fate. That didn't seem to take anything away from the cheers and celebration during the rolling credits once the screen went black.

At the end, Keith took to the stage, thanking everyone for their attendance, inviting them to stick around for food and drink. After saying his peace, he managed to vanish the room unscathed, congregating to the bar just outside the dark hole of a theater.

Eventually his film crew joined him there at the bar, sloshing drinks, bathing in their immediate success. On her way past the rush of theater goers, Keith's aunt caught a glimpse of him, making a bold move to brush past them.

She got enough of their attention to get a gaze from Keith. "Keithan!" She screamed. She searched for a reaction, but his only response was a glazed look on his face, his body remained still. He hadn't the faintest idea who she might be, although familiar, he kept looking, searching in her eyes, but he was in no mental state to

13

remember anyone he had barely met in his youth. Nobody called him by his birth name, hardly anyone knew what it even was. It was only a matter of time before he would make the connection. Whether it was her long curly hair, her hour-glass figure, her porcelain skin, or her undeniable smile; she was unforgettable. She didn't have any bags under her eyes or wrinkles like most women her age. She was a natural beauty, sad but beautiful, and familiar to Keith. It was only a matter of time before he would make the connection who she was.

That night, Rainor nearly got into a fight twice with someone who dared to taunt him. No one paid any attention to it, figuring it was just a jealous nobody wishing to get the best of him; but, Rainor took it personally, having to talk himself out of punching this guy's lights out. He often had to talk himself out of fighting. Notorious for being hot-blooded, there was a famous Old Harbor fight between him and two other brutes. After one had tried to make a pass at his girlfriend, Rainor knocked them both out, sending one of them to the hospital. Instead of getting any criminal charges, he was expunged of the incident, all-together. That's the kind of favoritism Old Harbor had for him, another reason why the underground youth fought to ride his coattails. The bloody mess and ambulance frightened Rainor, not sure what kind of damage he had done to his unconscious victim. Everyone was certain he was let off the hook by Old Harbor's police, thanks to his family ties. And, even though he was vindicated and admired for beating the two guys up, he learned a valuable lesson: never let a hot temper get the best of him. There was no telling what trouble it could get him in. So, when some sly nobody tried egging him on, he did everything in his power to calm himself down. This miscreant purposefully bumped into Rainor as everyone was meeting and greeting at the party.

Without extending his hand, he said, "Hey, how about me, do I get a handshake?" If Rainor was meant to take it the wrong way, he did, and he was furious about it. To think someone, he didn't even know would have the audacity to approach him in such a disrespectful manner put him in a rage. Trying to seem cool, he left the room, as gracefully as he could, without giving off any heat. He quickly stepped into the furthest bathroom and jammed the door shut. Pouring cold water on his face, he said to himself, "You're not going to fight this punk. You're not going to fight," he repeated over and over. As bad as he wanted to fight, this self-coaching worked for him. He was told to perform certain self-disciplinary actions like this. Anytime he felt the urge to fight, he could psyche himself out of it. It was unfortunate, but he was a fighter, and it was important that he never fight again because of the amount of trouble it would bring him and his family.

Still, that wasn't the only person wanting to pester and provoke Rainor… little did he know, he was being overheard and photographed by Sylver, the creep of the lot. An informer to a local gypsy and fortune teller, he was promised one night with one of her younger workers who was very beautiful. All Sylver had to do was dig up dirt on Rainor. She knew he was a prominent member of Old Harbor society. She was looking to sell out, to move out of her dumpy bungalow, and upgrade her life, by getting a juicy story to sell to the tabloids. The gypsy, Famima, doubled up as a spiritual healer for all the lost souls to whom she would tell a lullaby, focusing her eyes on their tiny hearts, putting them to sleep, and filling their heads with fantasies. She would also screw their brains out if she had to. Although, Sylver knew Famima was far from being a head madam, he was more than happy to do his dirt, because he was scum. So, he took pictures of Rainor with a spy lens camera.

Greedily, he snapped pictures, in a psycho flurry, pulling out his cell phone he had Famima on speed dial, "Yes…?" She answered. "He's bi-curious." He snapped, "I have the photos… he's teasing cock as we speak." This, of course, was outside of Rainer's nature as a straight-and-arrow guy. But, indeed, he was frolicking, as lads do, taking it further than he should have, due to his drunken state. "I want to see my present from you." Sylver said, ambitiously, "Show me the girl!" He demanded. "Not until you show me proof." Famima replied. "I have it, if not, then I will have you!"

"You stupid man. I lay everybody in this city. Just get me Rainer and you will have your present." She quickly hung up the phone, leaving him stupidly in the brush, alone, outside of the estate. All at once, Sylver realized what kind of a creep he was, if that was possible. That, however, did not deter him from continuing his weak ploy against Rainor, barely even able to hold himself together with his phone and camera weighing down on his feeble hands. These were his most prized possessions; and, this, was his most prideful accomplishment. He was a pitiful man, to say the least.

♣ ♣ ♣ ♣

The next afternoon Bollinger spent some quality time with his closest friends, and absinthe. The musketeers; Bollinger, Petit, and Leblanc, were all consuming in a dry, god-forsaken heat. Petit was the first to prod and so he provoked them, as he usually did, by flattering them like the proverbial Fox and The Crow. He set his aim on Leblanc and the innocent Bollinger.

15

"You know, LeBlanc... Eve asks a lot about you..." Said Petit.

"Oh yea? LeBlance answered. "What does she say, I wonder? She must know how close we are..."

"A lot of it is in jest, but she lights up anytime I mention your name. She's constantly dreaming, talking, dreaming... there isn't a rational bone in her body. But it's not what she says, dear Leblanc, it's the way in which she asks..."

"How do you mean?"

"Well, for example, anytime I make mention of a friend, no matter what, for whatever reason, she brings up your name."

"So...?"

"It's the way she responds..." A prolonged pause... there was no need for conversation anymore in this moment. Naturally, LeBlanc was interested in learning more.

"And so...?" He finally replied.

"LeBlanc, my dear friend, you should see her when she asks..." Petit paused again, catching his wind. "Like a fox on the hunt. She doesn't see it herself, it's all very reactionary, you see, a knee-jerk reaction, but she reacts so gently and coquettishly when I make any insinuation or mention of you. I'm not jealous, but the imagination she must have for you..." He turned away for a moment. There was nothing else to think about; they were in a state of wonder. Petit had a way of putting people in ultimate suspense, getting them to shun reality for a period of time. "The poor thing is always dreaming." He finished abruptly. He swirled his drink around in his hand, ever so carefully.

"You probably are wondering what she is capable of in bed, it's not like you haven't seen her. She is in fact nimble and cool, like a little nymph." LeBlanc hastily finished his drink. He nervously reached for the bottle to pour himself another glass.

Petit noticed his reaching, "You've finished your fifth glass..." He remarked. "What?" Leblanc nervously replied. "Not to worry, I brought more." He laughed in a jaunt, stoked by the irony of the situation, the ease of which he would be able to prey. It was hard to make out Petit's true character or intention, he was neither good or bad,

16

he was simply him. He was a representation, and a raconteur. He was carefully opening another bottle, when he looked LeBlanc straight in the eyes and said, "Isn't the familiar saying true? Sharing… is caring…?" Saying it so intentionally, Leblanc was caught off guard, livid from Petit's insinuations. "What are you saying?" He begged.

"Help me liberate Eve from her idle fancies, her fantasies…" LeBlanc was noticeably bothered at this point, his legs were too tightly crossed, he showed a very tight demeanor. "How?" LeBlanc answered, perhaps too eagerly. There was a pause. Petit held his position, quickly scanning with his eyes if he had induced a phallic reaction. LeBlanc couldn't fake an appearance of indifference quick enough towards this lusty proposition. His response was obvious, too short and too quick. They were completely out of their wits.

"What a great question. 'How...' well, it couldn't be anything too sudden, after all, I don't put her on to anything like this. Why would I? And, you know how embarrassing life gets when you ask obvious questions pertaining to sex and affairs. It would have to be something puts people at ease, in the right mood, but not overly secretive. That would leave me with nothing, you see?"

"You're not answering the question…" LeBlanc replied, overly eager, perhaps too suddenly. "What question?" Petit answered. LeBlanc was in a controlled state of panic, mentally decapitated. "How to have your, our, tryst…" "Ah, right, as to exactly how we should go about this? A key's party… of course…" "A what?!" "A key's party" Petit replied. He quickly glanced at Bollinger from the corner of his eye. Philipe was becoming very insulated, he seemed tepid hearing this. "A key's party?" Philipe asked. "Yes, between us… fair enough Philipe?" He saw Philipe's change in expression, after proposing his girlfriend to LeBlanc, but Philipe was not anywhere near being as comfortable with this level of promiscuity, especially since Sally was so dear to him.

Petit, on the other hand, had his girlfriend under a spell and would make his rounds with women as he wished, "I don't want to do anything like that," Philipe retorted.

"Listen, Philipe, I'll tell you this for your own good. One night like this, and your life change for the better. "I don't think so." Philipe replied. "Don't deceive yourself, what, do you want to settle down with your girlfriend, to never look at another girl again?" A settling silence left the air between them empty and dry, until Petit continued. "There's plenty more to learn from. Trust me. I'm telling you this

17

from experience. You enjoy romance, don't you?" "What's your point?" Philipe cried out. Petit slowed down. He was going to spoon-feed Philipe, who was not entirely sure. What Petit was about to share was simply astonishing, especially after their fifth round of drinks...

"My lucky ones, let me share with you a lesson learned from a mistress, an instructive one well older than myself, who gave me clarity about how quickly a woman yields to her own desire. Her pleasure impulses her heart as quickly as the blink of an eye. How quickly women yield to pleasure..." There was a clearing of air. Petit snapped his fingers. "Like that!" Sipping his drink in a fit, he recounted his story... "I met her at a University. She was a high school teacher, studying...God only knows what... Something extra that day. As she walked out of the classroom, she was a vision to say the least. Her eyes were like coals of fire, she exuded such energy, the type one gets from working with youth. She was on break, and as she caught a glimpse of me, she immediately pretended to be looking for the cafeteria. I concluded that was where she was heading to after class, but she couldn't hide it from me.

I approached her tactfully, not letting her see me approach her, yet remaining visible within the corner of her eye. After an exchange of pleasantries, soon I was walking side-by-side with her to grab lunch. I kept the conversation short and sweet, out of fear of committing a faux pas with such a woman. We had just met after all. And, my god, I was completely distracted, because she was undeniably beautiful, and voluptuous.

After a somewhat feisty exchange of small talk, we exchanged information on a friendly note, I concealed my lust, she pretended to be busy at work. She said she looked forward to speaking with me after I mentioned that I was studying at the University too.

Two days after we met, I contacted her over the internet, through instant messages. Mind you, this was the first time I had courted someone in an instant message. And, let me tell you... it was fast and a testament to how fast a woman loses her inhibitions. She was swift in replying to every one of my advances, it shocked me how quickly she responded."

"I texted something to the effect of... 'Nice to meet such a beautiful woman with such a profound interest in the sciences.' She took this compliment well, and soon we were engaging in a more livid conversation through instant messages. But later in the conversation I think she became afraid. This is something new to me... because this normally doesn't happen in person, normally it's the other way around...

18

after breaking the ice, a woman is ready to go... but I suppose she became intimidated knowing she was succumbing to sexual desire, without her gifts at work. After all, does a mistress not wish to instruct?

By then, I knew full well the risk I had to take to provoke her in such a way that I would succeed on the slightest of pretenses. I flattered and consoled her accomplishments as an experienced researcher. That was not hard, since it was all true. But I also gave her a hint. It was an invitation, to have sex... and wouldn't you know, she accepted, without shame!

A devilish smile shined on Petit's face. "My dear friends, you would not believe this, only if it weren't true. But it is, or else I wouldn't have believed it myself. I wish you could have seen her. Beneath her concealed looks, was a very gorgeous woman. I could have easily mistaken her for the prude, but she proved me wrong, so wrong..."

"... I began texting her in French, she only spoke a little French, not much. I asked her if she would like to learn. Yes, of course, she replied. I asked her in earnest, 'Voulez-vouz... ce soir?' Of course, implying if she would sleep with me that very night! Thanks to the bold song, I owe, because she had responded a thousand 'yes's' simply by replying, 'Ce soir? Non, merci.'

Their eyes were engorged with lust and fascination, Petit was like a volcano oozing red hot in the face. "And, so, I asked when. At this point she knew full well what she had responded to, and, she came to her senses...

'What do you want with me?' She finally replied...

"And what did you say?" LeBlanc asked.

"My God, you never would guess. It was so wrong, so totally wrong, but I don't know what happened, something got into me. You know, the privacy thing, the texts... it becomes like an addiction."

"What did you say?!"

"Really? Okay, I'll tell you... whether it was the rapid pace of the chat, or my pent-up lust. I don't know... but, honestly, it was bad.

"What? What did you say?" LeBlanc asked again.

"I… I…" Petit hesitated. He was tipsy.

"What?!" LeBlanc demanded.

"I told her… I told her to suffocate me."

A brief pause, before erupting in laughter, the laughs being sucked out of them, a rush of sin crept in. It was as if they had lost themselves, and were overtaken by a collective hedonic force.

"How rude!" LeBlanc roared. After regaining his consciousness, Petit joined in their laughter while he pressed his forehead, troubled. "What happened to her?" LeBlanc asked. "Did she try to keep you?" "It was a great one night stand, I have to say." Petit replied.

"You're a beast!" LeBlanc exclaimed.

Now, he was the one losing consciousness. "So, what about this party?" LeBlanc followed in a sudden shock.

"The party?" Petit asked.

"Yes… this key's party…" LeBlanc replied.

"Oh right…" Somehow he regained his composure. "It's like any other party… Invite who you like, and don't leave with who you came with."

Petit looked carefully into Philipe's eyes, seeing his trepidation and reluctance, Petit continued. "Think about it… imagine having any girl you wish, to have women begging to be with you… that's what this will do for you… After all, you don't want to be attached by the hip, do you? How long have you been with your now?"

"Around five years."

"You plan on marrying her?"

"I don't know, sometime…"

"What would you rather have, a wife who is eager to please you, or one who is always itching for an affair?"

20

"Neither."

"This will blow the cobwebs off your love life; and, believe me, it's liberation.

"How many times have you done this?" Philipe asked.

"A few… it's not like they happen often." Petit answered.

Philipe turned to LeBlanc. "How about you?"

"Two or three" LeBlanc answered casually.

"And…?"

"And he's right…"

"What about your experience, what was it like?"

"A couple drinks, some games, some fun afterwards, with someone else. No big deal, just meaningless sex." Philipe looked out into the fields; slowly, his mind was changing without him knowing it.

"How would I?" He asked.

"Tell her it's innocent fun, if she refuses, ask her if she's never fantasized about being with someone else, if she denies it, she's lying, and when she admits that she has, tell her that's it no different."

"Where do you plan on throwing it?"

"Here. My parents are gone until the end of the month."

"When?"

"What day works best for you Philipe?" He replied sarcastically. LeBlanc and Petit started chuckling mischievously.

Sylver rapped at Famima's front door, to deliver his dirt on Rainor and collect his bounty. As soon as Famima opened the door, Sylver lit up with a crocodile smile. She was surprised to see this beast, and appeared a little frightened of his ugliness, she was expecting her beautiful daughter.

"What are you doing here?" You were supposed to meet me at my business..." She said.

"I deserve a better welcome than that... after what I've done for you?" He shoved an envelope full of illicit pictures into her face. Her eyes lit up, but before she could say or do anything, Sylver took the liberty to step inside her house, which was more like a bungalow. It was an oddly familiar smell of incense, and spice coming from the kitchen, jammed next to the living room. They were nearly one and the same room. "Very nice place you have here... cooking something?"

"It's for my daughter... who should be home any minute now. You have something for me?"

"Yes, of course..." He replied. Slowly, he unsheathed the envelope, stopping before showing the pictures, "How is your daughter doing by the way?" He asked. She snapped at him, "Just show me the pictures." She said angrily.

Famima stared at him coldly, at his audacity, the fact that he was supposed to meet her earlier during work hours, and that he came uninvited, snaking his way into her house, made him audacious to her, and she was disgusted by him, but she didn't have time to sweep him out, especially not after he had brought the pictures framing Rainer, the pictures she would sell to gossip magazines.

Without hesitation, Sylver unsheathed the photos displaying black and white enlargements of Rainer at the party. Sylver closely guarded the photos like precious diamonds, he was stalling, so that maybe he could see Famima's daughter come home and perhaps oblige Famima to have dinner.

Sylver rambunctiously tried to explain the photos and what was happening in each shot, but she was growing tenser by the minute, knowing her daughter would be there any minute. She stood up at the first sign of a car motoring by.

"Ah, that must be her!" Racing to the front window, she hollered at him, "You must go now. Thank you!" But the car continued down the street mercilessly. She went outside hopelessly in search of her daughter, but she was nowhere to be found. It was just a blank street. Famima's next-door neighbors were in their houses having dinner with their families just fifty feet from where she was standing. As she

22

re-entered her house she noticed the pictures, and Sylver, were gone. At first, she was relieved, but then worried crept all over her as she faintly heard Sylver whistling in the bathroom. Storming over to the bathroom, she put her ear to the door in horror, she could indeed hear him, he was still there. She tried jamming the door open, but it was locked... "You need to leave. Now!" She yelled.

"I'm using your bathroom." He insisted.

Inside, he was selfishly shaving with her razor. Famima became furious. He wasn't supposed to be here at all, let alone, wasting her time; and now he was playing games with her by keeping the photos from her.

"Where are the photos?" She cried out.

"They're here." He said coolly. Immediately, she rushed into the bathroom to find the photos lying next to Sylver who was standing over the sink shaving.

"What are you doing? Get out!" She grabbed the photos and shooed Sylver out of the bathroom. At that moment he made his advance. Clasping her arm, he whispered, "Famima, you know how I feel about you." "Get off me!" She shouted. But he didn't relent, "What would a miscreant like me be without your love? Can't you see you drive me crazy?" His eyes darted into hers. "When I look into your sweet, caring eyes, I can't stand to think of the things you're willing to do with other men... but not me. How can I live knowing how you wish to devour Rainor? Oh, Famima, punish me, put an end to me!" He collapsed onto her, kissing her bosom like a feverish baby, but she backhanded him, hard, tossing him against the bathroom wall. "Get yourself!" She shouted. "I can't live another day knowing I might never be with you." He said, pathetically. "You're all I want. You're all I want to see." He wasn't letting up one bit.

"Let me just talk some sense to you Sylver, because, apparently, you've lost your mind... You're not a love interest of mine. You're not a client of mine. You weren't invited here, and you're getting on my last nerve, playing games with me, in my house, when you know full well you have no business here. It's time to go. You need to leave and never come back."

Sylver begged and pleaded for a moment, then she gave him an even more violent backhand, slapping him against the wall again. He looked sad and pathetic, completely defeated. "And get those ridiculous thoughts of me out of your head, you're the last person on Earth I would ever sleep with."

23

But as soon as she said this, Famima' s daughter made her way through the front door. As if the sun had just broke through the clouds, Sylver turned on like a light. He went from sad and helpless, to being suddenly alert. Without skipping a beat, he burst out of the bathroom attempting to expose himself and Famima, in front of her daughter. He knew full well Famima wouldn't let him do it, out of shame of their appearing intimate. So she abruptly shut the door, and locked herself in with Sylver.

"Everything alright?" Famima's daughter asked. It was obvious she was worried.

A cold change of expression in Famima' s face said it all, there was a chill. She was now completely trapped. Sylver knew he had all but won; looking over, she stood there, vanquished. He looked at her with the same amount of scorn she had given him. Famima' s daughter came now to the door. "Mom…?"

Sylver quickly turned on the running water from the showerhead. He approached Famima, giving her a coiled embrace, ravishing her with kisses, until she became breathless.

"You taking a shower?" Her daughter asked.

Watering in tears, she replied, "Yes, honey." She lost the will to fight. Sylver put his hands all over Famima, undressing her, now having his way with her in the shower. He knew he could get away with this, without any mention or complaint from her, his sin was paid for. All he had to do was leave the pictures at her house, which he did.

Rainor's father, who had recently passed away, was going to be recognized with a medal of honor from Old Harbor's Fire Department. He worked there as a fireman most of his life. Rainor needed a date for this ceremony honoring his late father, so he called an elite escort service; this was a first for him. He never had a problem finding a girlfriend, but he had a certain quality he was looking for that he believed most of the girls of Old Harbor did not have. He desired a girl with brains as well as beauty, a girl that could demonstrate her wits as much as show off her body. He told this to the escort service very plainly, and, without any hesitation, they assured him they could find the right girl, but for an added cost. That right girl was Gia, a gorgeous girl, and a high-end escort, she had it all, it just was a matter if she had brains because Rainor wasn't going to have a hard time with her looks.

At his father's commemoration, Rainor and Gia sat with his mother and uncle at the same table. The room was full of his clan mates, who also had relatives that served, and still serving the city of Old Harbor and its surrounding areas. In keeping with tradition, Rainor wore his father's ring, an heirloom, on his left hand. Although his tattoos were covered up, some of his clan mates showed theirs, all nearly identical. The clan's tattoos featured a cross Moline on their forearms, Rainor also had one, as well as his family name in old English lettering, it was written on his right calf. Rainor was covered and buttoned up to the hilt; all anyone could see was his blond shaved head and his piercing green eyes. The commemoration master of ceremonies was Old Harbor's fire chief. He commanded a strong, bold presence with a booming voice that swept the room as he was making his speech.

"Anyone who knew Gregor, knew very well what a great man he was. Fearless, ambitious, cunning, and rock-solid just like his father… now we're all here today to commemorate his life and his unwavering service to the city of Old Harbor as a fearless fireman, a veteran of the marines, and as the last patriarch of the surviving Scottish clan." The audience gave a roaring applause. He continued, emotionally raising his voice over the applause, "A group that has kept our families' interests at heart and stood up in those few circumstances where fighting was our only option." The audience again erupted in cheers and applause, some in the front rows gave a standing ovation.

"Now you might ask yourself; 'Where do we go from here?' After the patriarchs are gone and the traditions of old have faded away… Who can we trust?

Those of us with the fire in our hearts to serve and work to preserve life, liberty and the pursuit of happiness, need to create an even stronger bond, an even stronger union. Just like our parents, grandparents, and great-grand parents did. Where do we go from here? The answer is before us, here. As I look around the room, I'm reminded of the old patriarchs. I'm reminded of our strong tradition and persistence to stand tall. I'm reminded of a rock-solid union that we have had, and will continue to have… Without any further ado, I'd like to call up Gregor's son, Rainor. Won't you come up to the stage Rainor and accept this Medal of Honor for your father, still with us in spirit."

The audience belted out applause as Rainor stood out of his seat. He waved to everyone in the room. "Come on up here son." The fire chief beckoned him to get on the stage, Rainor looked like a giant, standing at 6'1," next to the fire chief. He extended his hand and went in for a hearty embrace. The fire chief grabbed the medal, pausing, he said out loud, "This is for Gregor, a great man and a hero… to answer the question: 'Where do we go from here?' The answer is here, all around us; it's our next of kin." Rainer bowed to receive the medal around his neck as cameras pointed and flashed in a frenzy of picture-taking. They shook hands and stopped for a moment as the world now revolved around them, a freeze frame that would make it to the front page of next day's local paper.

♣ ♣ ♣ ♣

Later that night, Rainor and his date, Gia, went to a local coffee house after their date to have a late-night bite and coffee. A couple of singer-songwriters were alternating sets at the café. The band was dedicating their last song as Rainor and Gia waited for their order. Gia didn't say much. She only spoke when spoken to, as a trained GFE escort, she was paid for the so-called girlfriend experience. Although there were few words exchanged between them, they were a very impressive couple to look at.

There was a lingering song in the background, Rainor couldn't help to think how meaningless the singer's lyrics were. Yet everybody seemed entertained. Nearby, was none other than the inglorious fortune teller Famima, finishing up someone's reading. She caught a glimpse of Gia and immediately recognized her, she was surprised to see her with Rainor, who she already had her sights on. Gia knew Famima from the brothel just outside of town where they had both worked. They locked eyes for a moment, Rainor couldn't help but to notice. "Who is that?" He asked, thinking he had seen her before, she looked familiar to him. "She looks like a fortune teller…" Gia answered plainly, concealing the fact that she knew who Famima was. A perplexed look, clearly he had never ventured into this café on a Friday night, because live music and fortune telling were the norm. "Yes…" She repeated while still looking at Famima, now counting her cash.

Rainor was momentarily distracted when the coffee came. Gia shook her head at Famima like she was a bad omen. Before Rainor could even sip his espresso, Famima stalked their table and began talking.

"Hello… you like me to tell you your fortune?" "Sure," Rainor replied. "You're someone special… yes?" She asked.

"Special? No, I don't know about that… what makes you say that?"

"Well, I'm a fortune teller and a psychic…

26

"You're going to tell us our fortune?"

"Of course, I can…"

He slipped her a $50 bill underneath the table, trying to be discrete. She gladly accepted the cash, without looking at it, she smiled and started, "First, you two are not close… not yet. You just met recently, yes?" Rainor was surprised by this knowledge. "Yes… how did you know?" Famima silently giggled. "You have a very good rapport, an understanding of each other." She said. "And you will grow closer sooner than you think. Rainer answered emotionally, "But, we're just on a date…" Famima continued, unaffected. "Little do you know, your destinies are about to change and be intertwined." Gia reacted with a look of satisfaction.

"Give me your hand girl." Gia reluctantly gave her hand to Famima who grabbed it and caressed it. "Oh, such beautiful hands. For someone with such soft hands you are very harsh, very brutal in what you are willing to do for money." Gia tried to relinquish, however unsuccessfully. "If you're not careful, your own fate and fortune will consume you. Rainor was impressed by her apparent expertise, but Gia knew she was referring to her work as a call girl and had heard enough already. She was giving Rainor the girlfriend experience, but unbeknownst to him, there was little Gia wouldn't do for the right price. Famima studied Gia for a quick second, who was looking back at her with scornful eyes. Famima continued in her spell. "After your night is over, you will be meet a man with a scar on his face and speaks like a snake. You know who he is, but you must flee from him because he will slowly destroy you, unless you destroy him, or run away. Rainor was completely reeled in at this alarming statement. "Who are you talking about? Who is this person?" He asked hysterically. She knew that Famima was referring to Gia's boss, but Rainor didn't know who he was.

A mysterious man began playing the Spanish guitar outside, which could be heard inside the café. "This man tells you where to go, and who to see." Famima said. "But he shows you no sympathy for the sins you help him commit." Rainor began guessing who this person might be. "Unless you choose to find your fortune elsewhere, you will be cursed by him as long as he's alive." Gia couldn't stand to look Famima in the eye any longer and looked down, but Famima brushed her face to keep eye contact. "You see?" Gia looked down again. "Look at me." Famima looked straight into her eyes, carefully, to make sure she understood. They exchanged a look. "Is that all?" Gia answered. "Yes… that is all."

♣ ♣ ♣ ♣

Gia was terrified to think of the work cut out for her after seeing Famima like this, how she would have to face all the angst and emotional heartache of having to sell her body into the night. If what Famima was saying was true—and she did believe she was being truthful, there wouldn't be any more girlfriend experiences for her, no more evening dinners, enchanting galas, or commemorations, and no more Rainor, who was quickly growing on her as a great catch and love interest. She had to think of a way to get in Rainor's bed and stay there, a task that didn't seem impossible with the talent she possessed. She would have to close the deal on Rainor so that he would fall for her as a girlfriend, not just a fling. It was true what Famima was saying; their destinies were about to change. Gia was not going back to licentious prostitution; no way was she going to become like Madame Famima. Not after tonight and the opportunity that lay before her.

It stood to reason that Rainor would want to remain her boyfriend, so long as she was giving him a free service, but she needed to land on more solid ground than that. And she knew, based on what he had said on the call, that he desired a woman with brains, which she had. There was just one major obstacle: she didn't talk much. Whether it was her Eastern European upbringing, or her protocol as a high-end escort, she was trained to be purely an object of beauty, not a pageant winner.

"Fa-mi-ma" Rainor pronounced out loud, looking at the business card she had left. The server swung by their table, "Can I get you two anything else?" Rainor looked at Gia who shook her head 'no'. "I'll get you your bill." The server then dashed away.

"It's funny, that fortune teller actually looks familiar to me. I wonder where I've seen her before..." Rainor said, ironically. She definitely had your number." Gia didn't respond. "I slipped her some cash if you were wondering whether I paid her or not..." The look on Rainor's face was Gia's guarantee that he didn't have the slightest clue who Famima was and Gia's relationship with her. "I'm getting cold baby." Rainor put his jacket around her. "Here," he said. "Can we go to your place?" She asked. The waiter entered with the bill. Rainor left some cash and tip. "Yeah, let's go."

On their way home in the car, they didn't say much, consumed by what Famima had laid upon both of them, until Gia said, "I'm glad I met you." Rainor turned towards her and gave her a somewhat absurd response, "Me too." He said. Gia kept silent after, letting him drive her to his apartment where she would devise a way to stay to become his main squeeze.

28

Rainor's apartment was remarkably clean with a modest amount of space; it looked like he was the only one living there. The two had a few moments drinking wine in front of the TV, this didn't surprise Gia, she was used to cuddling up to her few clients who ordered the girlfriend experience.

Once in his room, Gia had full control, seducing him in her lingerie, as he struggled to get his clothes off. She stood next to the light switch, "On or off?" She asked. "On," he said. This was the part of the night where Gia could take advantage, this was her profession. Without even questioning, she ripped open a condom lying on the dresser and discretely slipped it on him.

She was going to pull all the stops; her livelihood depended on it. If Rainor remembered nothing else that night, one thing was for sure; he wasn't going to forget the smell of sex dripping like oil off her body.

The next morning, Rainor and Philipe were in bed with their girlfriends, both in Old Harbor, both equally significant in their own respect, and both with the same male instinct of detaching. Gia and Sally both lied awake next to their men, both with the same intention to spend the afternoon with them, and both completely consumed by their cell phones in bed.

In the middle of Gia's furious dalliances, she noticed a text message to her surprise, it was from Petit. The subject header read, 'Petit Soirée', on her phone, with the message 'Spend the evening at the Petit wine estate with good company. P.S. Be excited to meet new friends for a ravishing good night!'

Her heart nearly jumped out of her chest, someone must have been talking her up, she thought, that she would receive an invitation like this. She had a mix of excitement and fury in her heart; this invite was quite a surprise. It had been a very long while since she had been to a 'soirée'.

A message from Petit like this meant a party in the hills with well-heeled people and the who's-who of the wine business. Since it was an invitation from none other than Petit himself, she knew this was one of his key parties.

Always presupposing himself as a master of seduction, Gia knew Petit better, she had first-hand experience from his parties. She knew how compulsive he was, and what a tyrant he was. The first key party that she could remember of his was in a hotel. Of the two she had gone to, this was the calmer one; and a lot more anonymous. One of the perks was no one had to drive home to finish the night; they simply went to an already checked-in hotel room with their lover. People were free to lounge and party as they pleased. And, although it was an unmemorable affair, it was even-keel and unemotional, which was always good for this type of affair. Then, there was the second key party she attended at the wine estate, an emotional roller coaster ride. Some had to leave because their lovers did not want to go through with the partner swapping. And some, including Petit, ended up losing money. Yet, it was a night Gia would never forget. One thing she remembered the most was leaving the mansion a little richer than when she had arrived. They played a game, wagering money for silly sexual favors. Gia rounded the bases at it, giving her first dibs at the key selection. She could vividly remember everyone's key chains, they were all so obvious and uniquely different with various gems and charms. One had been the keys to a Porsche, one had a guitar charm, another had a gem-encrusted skull with ruby red eyes. What she hadn't remembered —because she had had no idea—was how a filthy glass bowl like that could sucker-punch guy's hopes and dreams, and throw everyone in a tailspin. Their male emotions oscillated from worry—watching their girlfriend fish for another man—to excitement in anticipation of their choice lover picking them. The excitement waned and quickly turned to despair as those who were too timid or unlucky to pick early made the last selections, having to choose the last of the bunch. It had been a crushing experience, but Gia didn't feel it, until she had rejoined her boyfriend the very next day; it wasn't long after until they broke up. She had secretly blamed it on Petit, swearing she would never speak to him again.

'That bastard child,', Gia thought, he was the one inventing all this debauchery in Old Harbor. Gia wasn't aware of all the going-on's of uptown, and how it had been debased. They were just as hedonistic, if not more so.

Mixed emotions aside, Gia secretly rejoiced in this invitation; it meant she would have a chance to be a part of society again. More importantly, it would be her chance to land a boyfriend that could help her with her predicament: a life of prostitution.

Gia joined Rainor in the kitchen for a quick breakfast, first looking curiously around his apartment like a child would. She noticed a picture of him with some of his friends; it was a wild looking picture of him. "These your friends?" She asked.

"Fraternity friends…" he replied.

"Oh, college?"

"Yeah…"

"What fraternity?"

"All different ones…" He finished setting the table. As Gia made her way to the kitchen, she timidly tried to give him a look, one of hope and wanting. He didn't seem to notice how much she wanted him. She sat down to eat, carefully chewing her food, trying not to look directly at him, she could tell he was in a mood. "What college did you go to?" She asked.

"Military college." He said.

"Oh ya?"

"Yeah, I studied military logistics".

"Oh, that's impressive…" She fought back the need to explain herself and paused. "The way you are and everything."

He gave her a stern smile. "How about you? You go to college?"

"I did. I studied math… without a degree though…"

"No? Why not?" He dared to ask, and on second thought knew he probably shouldn't have.

"I couldn't afford it anymore…" Rainor looked sympathetically into her eyes, letting her know it was safe to talk. "Well, that's not entirely true. Actually, I completed all my coursework for a math degree. It's just…" She looked down, not wanting to say anymore. "My parents died in a tragic accident. So, I wasn't able to graduate." She put her head down.

"I'm so sorry." He said.

"It's okay, it was a while ago, and I got over it, I guess, I just… I got caught up a little… well I guess you figured that much." After a moment's pause, she looked at him like a lost sheep.

"Listen, if you ever need anything, you have my number. I'm here for you."

"Thank you." She squeezed his hand and put her head against his arm. "Can I give you a hug?" He asked. She nodded warmly. He got up and gave her a deep embrace. She could feel his heart racing. "Damnit Gia... I... I wish you all the best." He almost said 'I love you', but realized how foolish that would have been since he was planning to drive her home and may only wish to see her until the next call, and that would be that. Yet she knew what he was meaning to say. She liked him, a lot, but maybe they weren't meant to be right now, she thought. Or, maybe they were...

Rainor rushed to put the plates in the dishwasher and went to his room to get dressed. "What are you up to today?" Gia asked.

"I'm having brunch with my mom."

"Oh, that's nice! I'd love to meet your mom, what a pleasure!"

'It's with my mom...' he thought to himself. He sort of wrote her off as too desperate, rather than the intelligent woman of his dreams. "Well it's going to be kind of a long day for me, and I got to get you home."

She grazed his naked upper body with her hand. "You don't have to take me home, you know..." He looked at her, cautiously reading her eyes. "Don't you have...? Don't you need to get ready for the week ahead?" He replied. "Can I stay here?" She snapped back. "I'll have all the house chores done, I promise, and I'll be here when you get home." He got excited suddenly, thinking how he could have a fantasy wife with her, something more than he could have bargained for. He just looked at her with stars in his eyes. "I need to take some time off work anyhow." She added. That of course meant she needed to quit her work all together, but it was no mind to Rainor now, he was on a cloud nine and would not refuse her proposition. He didn't think of 'Damnit, I love you', just a minute ago, he didn't think of the fact that they had met just yesterday, nor was he aware of what kind of predicament she was in to be doing him the favor. He simply left her with a warm embrace and kiss; after that, she would lay in wait for him.

A couple rounds of sex, Philipe worked up the courage to pop the party question to Sally. To his surprise, she accepted, willingly. No need to ask secretive questions, or scratch the surface, Sally was game for a key party, and this bothered Philipe greatly. He had to see her in a different light now, maybe she wasn't the reserved person he thought she was after all. Maybe she was fixed on laying other men besides him, if she hadn't done so already. After she responded to what Philipe had thought was going to be a difficult question to answer, he just looked at her for a moment in disbelief while she was getting dressed to leave.

"What? That's it?"

"What do you mean 'that's it'? You're the one asking me…"

"I mean, you, you just answered 'yes' like I was inviting you to a family picnic…"

"You're the one proposing we should go. Shouldn't you be happy? I'm accepting without any argument, are you suddenly above reproach?

"Who says I'm above reproach?"

"Why would you ask, if you didn't want to go to this party yourself?"

"I didn't think you wanted to go…"

"But, don't you? Why must you accuse me of being wrong? It's your party Philipe… you asked me." She added. "Let's not go, maybe we're not ready for this sort of thing."

Now he was livid. 'Was their relationship that easy to belittle?' Philipe thought, 'Is this what it had come to? A key party was now a test for a relationship?' He wasn't taking any of this lightly and Sally could tell.

"I have to go, let's not leave on a sour note, sweetie." Sally pecked Philipe on the cheek as she left the room. "You know that I love you, don't you, you love me the same, don't you?" Philipe relaxed a bit, retreating from his anger as he walked her to the front door. "Yes… I do…"

"Say you love me then." She hugged and kissed him at the door.

"You know I do, Sally…"

"Say it."

"I love you. I love you, I love you, I love you."

"There." She smiled. Aren't you terrifically more happy now?" He read her eyes; he could tell to this day she was thrilled to hear him say those three words that made all the difference in the world. He was happy now. He couldn't deny it, but all he could do was watch her blow him a kiss, driving away in her luxury coupe.

♣ ♣ ♣ ♣

On the way to Sunday brunch with his mom, Rainor noticed Sally in her car. She checked him out at the turn signal. For a fleeting moment Rainor forgot who he was, one look at Sally and he was reminded of all the joyful moments he spent with her, and all the great women he had been with in the past. The ones that got away, the ones he longed for, and the ones that were just out of reach. But here was Sally, recognizable, seemingly without hard feelings, practically within arm's length. For the rest of the day she haunted his thoughts, like a cinematic vision.

When Rainor returned home, Gia was there, sure enough, waiting for him. She thought she was going to be his goddess, but his first impression of her upon returning was lackluster. It wasn't the same electricity they had when they had first met. There wasn't the same passion in her eyes, just the calm and collectiveness of a homemaker. Nothing could have turned him off more after his Sunday brunch, the vision of Sally permeating his mind. Plus, Gia was not a trained homemaker. That meant no dinner and only a cursory workout in the kitchen. If Gia was going to win him over as a housewife, she was going to have to be more practical. He liked her as a sex-craving animal.

When they made it to bed, not long after, she screamed his during intercourse, whimpering. But he was fantasizing about someone else, a combination of people; a highlight reel of sex fantasies. Instead of seeing the beauty in this creature that loved him—perhaps more than anyone—he only abstracted what he wanted in a consummate fantasy.

He nuzzled against her, kissing her neck, their eyes rolled back. He couldn't stop fantasizing about all the women he had been with and had a chance to be with. Gia brushed his hair, moaning in ecstasy, as he sucked on her now hard nipples. He finally had his long moments of lust and love extinguished when he kissed her open mouth. Losing control of who he was, or why, he just began to kiss her entire body while she was lying down, slowly working his way down to her inner thigh.

They released what seemed like a decade of chemical romance. It was a firework show. After their orgasm, Rainor started to experience an extreme post-orgasm come down. Gia was sitting pretty, lapping up a near victory in her conquest with her new beau. His first instinct was to detach from her, and, naturally, her first instinct was to latch on to him, she had just given a performance in bed, with intentions of keeping him.

When Gia proposed that they become a steady couple, she thought it would be impossible to refuse after such amazing sex. But, Rainor was detached, and his alibi was that he was regarded in society, and was supremely confident after being given affirmation all week in the wake of his late father. He was reminded of so many girlfriends he went out with that still were eligible and willing to be with him. And the whole approach Gia was taking in intimacy was not working for him, not at all. So, when they had their talk after sex, Rainor hesitantly declined to be a steady couple when she asked. She couldn't believe it, here she was free-of-charge, willing to be his blowjob queen, keeping her troubles out of mind and away from him, yet he still dared to refuse her, he even had the audacity to tell her he thought it best they see other people before going steady. This infuriated her. In the same way reality bites, the nature of their reality was taking its course. If he was going to pursue a normal life, an abstraction, she would have to fight to fit in the picture. Yet, she was cunning, with an ace up her sleeve to fight against his refusal, despite his measure of perfection he wished to attain. 'My little invitation to this key party will do the trick,' she thought. "So why don't we go to a party that I'm invited to?" She asked, describing it for him. He was a little bit taken by her delicate explanation, a glossy overview, without any of the vulgarities of the party—only the games, and the fantasy of hooking up with other people.

"Where?" He asked consummately. "One of the wine estates, near Annulet Road." "The French estates?" He asked. "They're not all French, but yes." She retorted. He was sold by her invitation, and all too easily.

♣ ♣ ♣ ♣

The Petit's estate was normally a vapid space, but tonight it was a host to young things. The bar, French '75-ish, full of bougainvillea in a Gallic setting, and the smell of lavender all around.

Petit's girlfriend, Eve, loved playing host, she also loved being seen with Petit, she fancied his charm, quick-wittedness, his manner of speaking, even his goofiness. However, she was more in love with him than he was with her. She was after fanciful things, versus Petit, a great hypocrite who put on fancy, pretentious airs,

35

but was after gaining more fortune and power as an heir in the wine business. He only pretended to be aloof and carefree.

Keith and his girlfriend Karma, Karma's BFF, Faith, and their friends, were all at the Petit estate wearing locks and keys around their necks. "Locks for girls… keys for boys." Eve put key lanyards around everyone's neck, including Gia and Rainor, who were shattered as she was late to the party. As she put the key lanyard around Rainor's neck; he asked about the fishbowl to put his keys. "No sweetie, take this, she gave him one of the lanyards. You'll have a chance to meet. Don't be shy. Your key unlocks someone else's key, you just have to find out who."

Rainor caught a glimpse of Keith's girlfriend, Karma, and their friends— Faith, and her boyfriend. Keith had a famous tattoo of a two-headed dragon lining his back, reaching up all the way near his neck. The inspiration for this tattoo was something of a mystery; he always said it had religious references.

Karma also had many beautiful tattoos, most of which were new school tattoos. She had a tattoo of the face of her mom inked on her neck in her honor, her mom had died when Karma was a little girl. She held certain things precious, such as her mother's legacy. In a world of sacrilege, she still knew what was true, and that was of ultimate importance.

'One of the crowd here,' Rainor thought. Ironically, he was considered next of kin as the patriarch, whom his cousin, Keith, and his entourage, had much respect for. He was a whale in comparison, but here he was forced to swim in the tide pool as an equal.

Gia nudged Rainor, "I'm going to get a drink. Are you okay?" "Yes, I'm fine." He replied. But he was stuck, swimming in his head, thinking about the pariahs who would devour him if they had the chance. He forgot all this when he locked eyes with Sally. She put him in a trance. His fantasies with Gia had nearly vanished—his worries, vanquished. It was the most basic instinct between him and Sally.

After making a couple rounds, Gia had caught LeBlanc's eye. He was tending to Petit's alcohol feud that flared up to the point of no return after getting drunk from absinthe. He was singing "La Javanaise" in French, belting it out, hiccupping all over. Without hesitating, Gia approached LeBlanc to see if he had the key to her lock. She held out her key, "Do you want to try?" She asked. "Of course," He put his key in her keyhole, Petit nearly toppled onto both, spilling his drink everywhere, including Gia. "My blouse!" She shouted. "I'm sorry, so, so sorry. It's alright everyone, I've got it." Petit said, vainly. LeBlanc pulled out a handkerchief and dipped it in some water. "That's okay, I can get it off." Petit started cleaning up the mess he made, continuing to belt out the song like a madman.

"There, that should do it, it's out."

"What was he drinking?"

"A few shots of absinthe already, but he's drinking the same stuff,"

"Ol'e Delight?"

"Yeah."

She looked at her glass curiously. Petit went outside, whistling.

"Tell me your name again…"

"Gia."

"Gia! That's right, I've seen you a couple times before, haven't I?"

"Yes, you have. I remember seeing you too…"

"You have a pretty name."

"Aww, thank you."

"So how have you been? I haven't seen you in a while."

"Alright…

"Ya, really?"

"Well…"

"You can be honest with me…"

"Honestly? I'm in a bind." She paused after saying this. He hadn't quite earned her trust.

"Oh…?" He replied, non-judgmentally.

Eve rang her cow bell from the foyer, loud enough so everyone could hear. "Alright everyone, I'm glad you made use of your locks and keys. Now we're going to play a few games to break the ice. Oh, and please feel free to any drink you like, since it is an open bar. Philipe snickered under his breath. "Yeah, we noticed..."

"Okay, so we can start off with charades, or Pictionary, with which shall we start? There was a pause. "Okay, it looks like we might not be ready for charades yet. How about Pictionary?!" She looked around. "Where's Petit? Where ever is my boyfriend? Have I lost him already?" Petit was outside ogling Karma who stormed inside as Eve had gone out. "Oh, there you are! What are you doing my love? We are about to start playing." "I was... tending the wine cellar Cherie, I had just stepped out a moment. "We have wine..." "Yes, of course, but there can never be enough wine Cherie." "Come in now, you fool, we're about to play." He waltzed into the mansion, highly animated. "We are playing charades again Cherie?" "No, my love—." He began laughing, hilariously acting out a rooster, hiccupping all over the place. She tried to talk sense into him, but he didn't miss a beat in his own personal, animal charades. "We're playing Pictionary, my love." But he didn't stop, he kept acting as a cow, then a rabbit.

In a quiet tone, LeBlanc asked Gia, "How's it going so far?" "Fine," she said. "I'm doing just fine..." She repeated. Here was a chance for privacy between LeBlanc and Gia, he grabbed her and led her outside to talk. "So... what's going on with you...?" "I was going to say... well I'll just say it. I'm at the end of my rope. You might know, or may not know already... I work as an escort—" "No, I didn't know that." He replied. "—And, I've been doing well for the last couple months, but I no longer have as many clients as I would like or need. And I don't want to be kicked on the streets to pay my bills." "I think I understand..." He replied, an involuntary grin written on his face. "What do you do exactly?" She searched in his eyes for a moment. "I accompany high-end clients to special events and dates. "Oh, yeah?" "I offer companionship... and if they want more, then I spend the night, as their girlfriend. "I see... who are your clients?" Right after LeBlanc asked this, Keith and his friend joined them outside to have a cigarette. "All types... all types... yep... so, what kind of car do you drive?" Gia asked. "Tesla..." He responded. "A silver Tesla." "Show me." He pulled out his keys attached to a magic 8-ball amulet. "Oh, it's true... ah, a magic 8-ball, let me try..." She asked, "Will I get lucky and find a new boyfriend tonight?" She shook the 8-ball, turning it over, it said, 'My sources say yes.' It read. "Oh, I hope so...!" She quickly handed him back his keys. "That's good luck!" He replied.

Inside, they played Pictionary, Karma drew a cross on a white board, She drew it very carefully. It was apparent that she knew what she was doing, Karma guessed first, "Iron cross." She exclaimed. "Close." Eve said, encouraging her to keep guessing. She began to emphasize the cross with different color strokes. Philipe guessed a cross Moline. "Yes, you got it. Nicely done!" She threw the pen back on the board. Eve went to see her Pictionary word from Petit. As she glanced at it, she was surprised at how difficult it was, "Oh my heavens, this is a tough one. How ever, will I draw this one?" She began by grabbing a gold and red marker, she drew little fleur-de-lys flowers. After the third flower, Rainor finally guessed a fleur-de-lys. "Close". Everybody swigged their glasses of Old Harbor Lights, joking about how ridiculously difficult this game was becoming. After LeBlanc entered the room, Eve asked him if he had a guess. She baffled another word. "Any guesses?" The white board was nearly full at this point. LeBlanc stopped for a minute, "Fleur-de-lys?" "No." She giggled, "That's what Rainor guessed already." "Give me a hint..." LeBlanc asked. "Yes, okay, it's a coat of arms." Karma downed her glass, slammed it on the coffee table. "House of Valois." A moment of reckoning filled the room, it was an abrupt acknowledgement, somehow everyone knew she was right before Eve could even say another word. She had known it all along, after Eve's drawing of the third flower, but didn't want to reveal her prescient knowledge. "Well yes! Very good Karma!" Again, Karma was careful and polite. "That was a tough one." "Great work!" Eve exclaimed. "Thanks." Karma replied as she got up to meet her friend Faith outside. "Cherie, we're giving everyone a headache." Petit exclaimed. "Hold on for me one minute I am going to get the couple's desserts, okay?!" Petit turned on some music with a touch of a button, they somehow managed to have a modern digital surround sound in this stodgy chateau.

Outside, Karma lunged at her girlfriend Faith, drinking absinthe. "So, my dear..."

"How ya doin'?" Faith interceded.

"I'm good."

"Whose key do you have?"

"I got LeBlanc." Karma replied. "You?"

"Oh, Petit, that old bore, he's no fun to talk to. Drunk ass." Faith looked at her for a second. "What a waste." She said.

"Whatever you say, dearie. Now will you trade with me or not?"

"Have it." Faith replied, "I don't want him."

Petit was in the kitchen with his girlfriend, preparing chocolate-dipped strawberries. Lapping up some hot melted chocolate with his index finger, burning his finger. "Ouch, it's hot!" He shouted. "Be careful," she said, but he wasn't paying any attention to her. "Wait until it's done." She added. Still deaf to her heeding, he tried dipping one of the strawberries, creating ruffles, he held it up. "Open up, Cherie." But she shook her head, 'no', forcing him to plead and give her his precious words and worship, as he so often did with her. "I noticed you made the cream, and the desserts are so perfect Eve, but you know what I want more than cream?" "What is that, my love? What do you want?" She moaned. "I want you", he said. "You know why?" "Why is that Cherie?" "Because I love cream so much." "So, then what do you need me for if all you love is cream?" "Because you're the crème de la crème." Satisfied with his answer, she finally sucked the icing off his finger.

There was no reason to be with him, he was pestilent, rude, cruel at times, sometimes foolish, and always conniving, a philanderer. But he was a dream, he made his passion known, and his passion for her was the greatest. It was an understatement to say they had something between them. He wouldn't have love without her.

The chocolate on the strawberry had hardened, Petit pressed it against Eve's lips, closing her eyes she bit into it. "Oh, so good…" She said. Petit kissed her and worked down delicately to her neck. "Stop it." She laughed, "Stop, I have to bring this to the living room. She held a plate of strawberries, arranged with fresh peaches and wrapped popsicles. "Stay with me a moment longer Cherie." He hiccupped. "You're drunk, my love." She replied. He grabbed her butt abruptly as she brushed past him, his tray in hand, quickly stepping out of the kitchen. It was a long walk back to the living room.

All the couples paired up in this now comfortable, loving, living room. It was Karma and Petit, Faith and LeBlanc, who was assured he had a new date. LeBlanc, still not sure what had happened, didn't realize that Faith had traded locks with Karma. The rest of the couples ended up being Keith and Gia, Rainor and LeBlanc's girlfriend—Roxy—and, finally, Philipe and Sally—still together by chance.

"First we'll have the chocolate strawberries." Eve announced. "And remember, this is all based on performance, so the winning couple will have the prestige, as well as receive a surprise gift. "Philipe, do you want to start?" "Sure," he replied. "What do you want me to do? "Grab the dessert, sweetie." He took the strawberry like he was about to eat it. "No, don't eat it. Give it to Sally." "Okay…" He replied. He looked at Sally once and put the strawberry in her mouth. She closed her eyes, taking a juicy bite. Before she could savor it, he asked how she liked it. She loved it. "Give it to me." She said, opening her mouth again. She took the whole strawberry. "Yum." "What do you all think?" Eve asked. The room was in agreement, very yummy.

"Who's next?" Eve asked. LeBlanc gestured with his hand. Without hesitating, he grabbed a strawberry and flew it in the air like an airplane, lightly, he pressed it against Faith's lips smudging chocolate on her. Still, she swallowed the whole thing. "Okay, we're up now." Petit said, anxiously licking his lips. "Wait Cherie, we have to judge their performance. "Everybody…? Anybody?" No one answered. "I thought it was nice." Petit said. "Karma?" "It was okay…" She replied. "Just okay?" "Yeah, it was alright…" "Alright," Petit prodded, "my turn?" He brought the strawberry near Karma's face. "Open your mouth." He said. Karma opened, tilted her head back to receive the fruit, he brought the strawberry closer to her lips, grazing her lips gently. It just dangled near her mouth. She didn't bite into it, just kissed it. Then, Petit pulled the strawberry back, teasing her some more. Everyone's attention was on Karma now. It was a moment that could have been a photograph, it was too long, but it was mesmerizing.

Finally, he gave her the strawberry. Her full, luscious lips enveloped the strawberry, she only bit off a small portion of it, making a sucking noise. A grunt of satisfaction escaped Keith who couldn't help himself, he was taken by the seduction. As for Petit, he had also lost his mind. It seemed he was the one being teased now, and it was safe to say, there was seduction in the room. Irritated by her boyfriend's teasing, Eve continued and asked the room, "How was that, everybody?" They were all bothered, Karma smacked her lips. In a delayed reaction, not to be rude, they simply acknowledged her politely. It wasn't distasteful, but just wrong enough not to say anything. Eve gave Petit a scornful look. In case he thought he was in the clear, he most definitely wasn't. Karma didn't like the fact that she was pissing Eve off, but she was feeling good about her near victory. "Alright, who's next…? Keith?" "I think he's next" Keith said, pointing to Rainor. "Alright Rainor…" Eve prodded. Rainor and Keith both looked nervously at one another, until Rainor hastily grabbed a strawberry. Without getting a good hold of it, he plopped it into Roxy's mouth, in such a way that she had to bite into it, forcefully. "Ah, these are tasty!" She said as she chewed into it. "What do you say, 'yes'?" "No, sorry, I don't think so." Grey quipped. "Alright, my turn." Keith grabbed the strawberry, plopping it in Gia's mouth. She sucked the whole

41

thing until kissing his fingers at the stem. Rainor shot her a look, completely smitten by her now, he was wishing he had kept her as a date and fantasy housewife. He finished the last of his champagne and hastily turned to the bar for more. "That was very, very good." Petit said. "Yes, so good we may never have to leave here." Eve said testily.

Petit glimmered, unintentionally showing his desire for Karma, he normally would say something to Eve, but he didn't peep a word. Eve just scoffed at his impertinence, feeling scorn for him. "What shall we do next?" She asked. The group just looked at each other, sipping their drinks. "I know... since the girls went first, how about we have the boys go first this time, and give them a chance to play?! She pointed to the desserts. Everyone looked at the plate of fresh peaches and popsicles. "Who wants to go first?" "What are we doing?" Philipe asked naively. Eve gave him a look of sympathy, she looked at the plate, and back into his eyes. He saw how she was looking at him, it was like seeing her for the first time. "You want to go first sweetie?" "Yes, of course." He smiled. Philipe slowly grabbed a peach and kissed it, still looking at Eve. He turned to show her his profile, directing his performance to her; he closed his eyes and sucked on the peach intimately, before taking a delicious bite. The ripe peach, soft enough to squeeze in his mouth made a slurping sound. He looked up at Eve again, as if requesting her approval. This was satisfactory enough for her, so she turned to Sally. "Yes?" Sally acquiesced coyly, looking down. Eve handed LeBlanc a peach. He squeezed it a little, and made too much juice squirt out, Gia pretended not to notice him, yet still looking out the corner of her eye.

On Keith's turn, he confidently grabbed a peach and slobbered on it, biting into it without closing his eyes. Gia looked away for a moment, not at all pleased with his performance. Last was Rainor who took a big bite of his peach in a similar fashion as Keith, except he knew not to make the mistake of keeping his eyes open. "Okay, very good. What do we think? Who won this round?" Eve asked. "Philipe," Karma interjected, "Do it again." "Aw, she likes the way you suck a peach." Eve retorted. LeBlanc and his girlfriend hastily sipped their drinks and looked at each other curiously.

"Any volunteers for the next round?" Eve asked affectionately. "For the girls, round..." Gia volunteered confidently. "I'll go." She said. Slowly, she unwrapped a popsicle. All eyes were on her now, she rubbed her lips against it, her lips becoming ice cold. She just kept her eyes on Rainor, not looking away for one second. He had lost his mind again, afraid he made a mistake by going to this party, and not securing Gia as his girlfriend. She was the most sensual, clearly in her element once and for all.

One thing was for sure, she made the room feel a lot more erotic, a better change then the tepid chill they were feeling just a moment ago. Yet their comfort level was soon going to change, because they still had to endure the sucker-punch of that nasty, filthy keys bowl.

♣ ♣ ♣ ♣

Petit carried the bowl around, it had a lot of appeal at first sight, but was quickly able to crush people's spirits. "Alright gentlemen, keys in the bowl, please. Better now, soon I'll forget…" He said as he passed it to everyone to put their keys in. This meant the couples would have to swap couples a second time. Keith was petrified, just a second ago he had a sure shot at sleeping with Gia. He had been fixing on this single expectation the minute they started playing. LeBlanc, on the other hand, was excited; he had another shot at someone else, perhaps Eve, who he was sure wanted him. It was quite a change of heart to say the least, considering just a second ago he was contemplating running out with his girlfriend with their feelings still intact.

The buzz from the party was sucked dry after everyone realized they had to swap partners again. The beginning of the party was unnerving enough to begin with. Philipe began to feel the discomfort he had when Sally first decided to go to the party.

"For our couples' dessert game, we have the surprise gift. Gia, since you won, you have your choice, darling, a guest pass with us at the Annulet Chateau, or first pick?" "Oh, definitely first pick…" She replied. "…Not that I don't want to be your guest." "That's quite alright darling; we can give our guest pass to Keith since he was on your team." Petit gave Keith a wink.

Karma traipsed over to her boyfriend Keith, kissing him all over. "Well done sweetie!" She exclaimed, she embraced Petit and Eve in jubilee. "We'd love to." Karma exclaimed.

"Go ahead and make your pick, my darling. And good luck." Gia stepped in front of everyone to pull the first key out of the bowl. Nerves were tense as she put her hand in the bowl. "And no peeking…" Eve admonished. Gia closed her eyes, fishing around the bowl with her hand for a moment, she could feel LeBlanc's magic 8-ball. Once she felt it, she fished it out by the ball, dangling it in the air for everyone to see, knowing full well whose keys they were. "That's me!" LeBlanc said. He galloped to Gia and took her by the arm and quickly out the door.

43

"Okay, who's next?" Eve asked. "I'll go." Faith said. She had no problem volunteering, since she had already worked up the nerve, knowing her advantage at being quick on the draw. Blindly, she fished her hands in the bowl, soon picking out a pair of keys. It was Philipe's, she knew whose they were just by feeling them. She scooped them out and showed it to everyone. "And whose are these?" Eve asked. Philipe flicked his hand up and got out of his seat, he kissed Sally sympathetically and walked to Faith, still jostling with Karma. She whispered ecstatically in Karma's ear. "I'm going out with Philipe, isn't that just peachy?!" After they left, it was Sally's turn, she looked at everyone, feeling a sting of anxiety. It wasn't as exciting as before when Sally didn't have to think about it. Plus, her boyfriend had just left the party with someone else, and now she was feeling the emotional comedown. Naturally, she had become crushed, alone and afraid. After a prolonged hesitation, she fished her hands in the bowl to pick out who she would leave with that night. And, it was going to change their lives forever.

LeBlanc and Gia went for a joy ride on their way home in his shiny silver Tesla. They barreled down Annulet Road for a late-night bite with hardly a soul on the promenade, just the pristine garden and landscape, a colorful medley of lit up bougainvillea. They walked into a casual pizzeria that was about to close to grab some Italian ice. For change, the restaurant cashier handed them silver dollars, for no apparent reason other than his curious interest in them, it wasn't every day that he saw this hot of a date in Old Harbor. Provocatively dressed, they reeked of sexual promiscuity. When they left the pizzeria, there was the noise of cats fighting in an alleyway. They waltzed up to a fountain. Perfectly lit up, they sat there eating their ice cream. "It's kind of creepy here late night." LeBlanc suggested. "Yes, but still so pretty." Gia replied. "How long have you lived here?" LeBlanc asked. "All my life." She replied, "You?" "Off and on, I would say 15 years now." A short pause, and then he followed, "I went to boarding school in Switzerland for most of my schooling, went to University, and then moved back here to help with my family business." "That's nice of you. Wine business, right?" "Ya... from cultivating to exporting" He replied.

An injured cat bounced towards them, crying off its pain, grazing against Gia, and then licking its wounds. "I might be able to help you out with your whole predicament..." Gia looked at him with hopeful eyes, "How so?" She asked, interested in what offer he might have for her. "Well, if you're willing to put in a little work, we could use a good host and bartender for our wine tastings. That would give you a place to stay at the vineyard as well." "Oh, that would be wonderful. I would love that!" She exclaimed. He smiled. "Let's make a wish." He pulled out two silver dollars, handing her one. She grabbed the silver dollar tightly. "Ready?" He asked. Hastily, she started to speak, "I wish I—." "No. What are you doing? He interjected. "What?" "You're not supposed to wish out loud." She looked at him in wonder for a fleeting moment and made her wish as they flipped their coins in the fountain. "C'mon." He said. He embraced her and quickly took her to the car.

Cutting through the shadows, Sylver appeared at the fountain. The stray cat purred and moved towards him, a familiar phantom of Old Harbor. He reached into the wishing well, scooping the coin out, he turned it from tails to heads, "Two sides to every coin, as it is with every wish…"

The next day, Rainor asked Petit to write a poem for him, for Gia, while the iron was still hot. Petit was known to be gifted in writing, even more so than in his ability to speak and cajole. After Rainor confessed his passion and love for Gia, Petit assured Rainor he would write a worthy poem for her. It was a big mistake for Rainor, however, to put his trust in Petit, who had ulterior motives.

That same morning, Gia woke up with a terrible premonition from a nightmare, she instinctively went to Famima's, another error in judgment. She too, somehow, someway, was becoming influenced. She became highly superstitious whenever her emotions ran wild like this, and so she fled heedlessly to Famima's.

Famima had hoped that Gia was in a better place by now in her life, but seeing Gia in this state was telling, right away Famima knew something was off. Frantically, Gia demanded to know more of her previous night's dream.

A few minutes after the fortune telling, Gia couldn't take it anymore, she called Rainor, in a panicked state, crying out over the phone, "I had a terrible dream." "What is it?" Rainor asked. "I had a really bad dream," She screamed. "That somebody wants to kill you." "What?" "I'm scared. She yelled. "I only have these premonitions so often, and it was so vivid, something is wrong, I know it." "Calm down, Gia, it was just a dream. You probably had too much to drink, that's all. Where are you?" "I'm at the fortune teller's, Famima's, remember?" She cried out. "She's telling me the same thing." He became curious, recollecting his own dream, similarly frightful. He wrote it off as an alcohol induced nightmare, not a premonition; he didn't believe in such things, especially not when under the influence. "What is she saying?"

He asked. "This isn't normal." She urged. "You know I don't think—." He tried reassuring her, but she insisted. "—I'm really scared Rainor. Please come, please." She pleaded. "Where is it?" He asked. "The city limit." She replied. "Keep driving until reach the city limit divider, on the left. You can't miss it." "Okay." He replied. "I'll be there as soon as I can."

Racing over to the brink of Old Harbor, Rainor had no idea Famima had been expecting him, sooner rather than later. He found the desperate fortune teller's place at the corner of the street—the city's limit, like Gia had said. He couldn't help but to think the worst, on his way over there, he noticed something was in fact not right, his mind was reeling. They were committed to sin from the Chateau, and now were in a spell of some sort.

The fortune teller's was in the middle of nowhere, one of few structures at the city's edge. It was easy to spot Gia in that tiny space, once inside. He gave her a tight embrace. The hug lasted a little bit longer than usual, he whispered in her ear to relieve her, he could tell her emotions were running high. Famima looked him over, studying him, as if to say, 'You know who I am? I know who you are…'

As Rainor sat down, she started with his reading, all too soon. "You have an easy fortune to read." Famima said. "Wait, what are we doing? I thought this was between you and Gia?" "No, this is about you too, I can help you, but I must perform my reading first…"

She looked deep into his eyes, scanning his face and body, almost as a game of charades, to put him in a trance, but also to maintain her control of the situation. After all, this was her business, and they were clearly under the influence. "I see you have fallen into sexual temptation." She started. "This is cause for weakness in your life." She paused for a moment. "You've been exploring your sexuality with other people… including other men." Confused and put off, he turned to Gia, "I thought this was serious." He said furiously. "I thought you said something was going on?" "Someone is conspiring against you." Famima said. "Conspiring…? Who?!" Famima tilted her head, still gazing at him. "That's a mystery." She said. "You can't know that, it's dangerous for you to try to learn more, or to pursue this knowledge. Just continue to explore the goodness in your life. As long as you stay away from temptation and sexual sin you will have nothing to fear." Still put off by Famima's warning, Rainor was obviously disturbed by her appearance of omnipotence in his personal life. It seemed odd and made-up to be a predicament for him.

Petit was the last person he suspected as untrustworthy. Yet, Petit still intended to cruelly make Rainor's poem an opportunity to drive his own selfish ends. Writing furiously at the Chateau, he was smoking an unbelievable amount of opium, from the night before, Petit began to think of Karma, who he was with at the Annulet Chateau. In an inebriated haze, Petit sat, pen in hand, and continued writing.

'Sweet beauty, sweet blesséd, hear my heart's request, to stop my heart's duress... bleeding to be near yours, forever pressed against you, where love is unopposed... where love is yet condoned. Sweet blessed be mine...' After penning the first couple lines, Petit took a break, smoking a bit more, he recollected his thoughts.

Penning the rest of the poem put him in a fix, it was an asphyxiation, an extension of himself, no longer a process, or a thought, 'Sitting at your footstool, to be near you, dreaming of you, loving you in secrecy, needing your intimacy; I'd die, making love to you, to remember me, so we could make love again, in a memory.'

He was sometimes caught in a stupor, and oftentimes vain, from the opium. He had lost himself in his writing, because his endgame wasn't necessarily beauty or lust, it was to control Philipe, already in his clutches. Ironically, penning the verses was his only escape. By sending the poem addressed to Philipe's girlfriend, instead of Gia, he would entrap Philipe, making him smitten of their supposed love affair.

As ill-intended as it was, Petit honestly didn't think much of it, he thought if Philipe could handle this kind of advance, he would be able to handle any scandal. This was just another notch in his belt, which he could brag home about. Philipe would end up thanking him, after Rainor had been put in his place. So, he thought. But that was the only justification Petit needed to make a masterful blow against Philipe on Rainor's account. It was purposefully cruel, the sort of malevolence that fueled him. What made it worse was how well written the poem was, in perfect calligraphy, able to cut diamonds in half a page.

Most of the people in Old Harbor had gone on vacation, only LeBlanc and a few notables stayed, it was the slow season for wine trade, but the LeBlanc's were now supplying most of the wine. The Bollinger's and Petit's estates had incurred major losses, being forced to dump millions of dollars' worth of wine, due to its going past its prime. The LeBlanc's decided they would continue to supply their bad wine worldwide, since no one had bothered to notice or at least hadn't spoken about it yet. Ironically, their success was increasing, Old Harbor Lights was becoming more of a rage, bringing in tourists from all over—the people gloated over their shiny wine flutes, commenting on how great the wine was.

47

Everyone who had returned from their vacations, came back to a new Old Harbor. It was like a cultural time bomb had gone off. Many of Old Harbor's paintings were breathing new life with heraldic themes and various other monarchic themes, one freakishly depicting the heraldry of the House of Valois. One piece, by an uptown painter, was a particularly bold and provocative mural-size painting. It depicted a naked man wearing a jeweled coronet standing next to a naked woman in a room lined with gold fleur-de-lys painted walls. They were portrayed licking the fleur-de-lys walls. The naked woman wearing a Valois head-dress, and the two of them held wine flutes in their hands. It became a popular painting, selling at a very rich price.

After Sylver and Famima sold the photos of Rainor to local tabloids, he was shamefully exposed in the gossip publications. Unfortunately, word spread quickly in Old Harbor's grapevine. Adding to Rainor's injury in the gossip columns, he was being bombarded with media flack, and neighborhood gossip about his suggestive photos and frolicking at Philipe's debutante party. The headline read, "Rain or Shine? Is This Still The Son? Rainor exposed at Old Harbor party." Adding insult to injury, the magazine featured a contrived interview of Philipe speaking his mind of what he thought of the sept clans. In the column, he was reported as saying, "To be honest, I don't concern myself with them, from what I know, the clans of old are being consumed by something very conflicting. Their business is their own… they certainly have no place in Downtown Old Harbor."

It wasn't so much the flimsy tabloid gossip, but the reverberations in such a small city that personally infuriated Rainor so badly. His good name was being defamed, and he was starting to painfully understand the mysterious conspiracies against him, that he now believed were true. But the worst was yet to come for him in Old Harbor.

Everywhere Rainor went, gossip reverberated back to him, it was a terrible noise that he couldn't escape, even people who normally said nothing seemed to coo and hiss at him. He had spent that week by himself and it was pure torment, spending most of his time indoors. When cabin fever set in, he reluctantly attempted a low-key outing, but was still being smeared by everyone who saw him. He stuck out like a sore thumb in Old Harbor now. He started to think he was losing his mind, not used to this amount of negative attention. The more people learned of him, the more he was fearful of what would be exposed of him. It was the only time Rainor felt the need to leave Old Harbor, for good, before he was ushered out of society.

♣　♣　♣　♣

The letter Petit wrote to Sally, supposedly from Rainor, arrived to her with the initials signed R.G. It was no mind to Philipe—even though she seemed infatuated by it— until Petit planted the seed of jealousy in his mind. Petit plainly told him in a bold-faced lie that Rainor and Sally were having an affair. He had no idea it was a love letter, but when Petit told him outright that they were having an affair, Philipe believed it. He began recounting their conversations, the letter was now a sure indication that they were cheating behind his back. His thoughts were racing, 'They were seeing each other after the keys party, it was more than meaningless sex...' He thought to himself. This made him red hot. So much so, he began to arm himself, he had lost control of his thoughts, he was prepared to end this altogether, so he started carrying a concealed weapon on him at all times, just in case things got out of hand. His gun made him feel secure, but he intended to do damage. With a weapon, he knew he could unleash fury on anyone, even someone as strong as Rainor. He even began to make short trips around town, running errands, still with his concealed weapon, it was a silver shooter, almost a museum piece, but it helped him regain confidence because he was losing it. He would drive around with different people in different cars; in Sally's white Lexus; in his black Maserati; and in a big truck he used for hauling goods around for work. Most of his time at home were spent in a frenzy of broken conversations on the telephone and obscenities. He had to always be out, to regain his footing, he could hardly talk to Sally in this psychological state. Yet, he was stoic, this injury brought out admiration for him, people were enthralled by his showing through downtown, passing through downtown, most knew who he was as an Old Harbor heavyweight. He was recognized as a well-educated, well respected guy, but he was captivating people's attention, people were talking about him, he looked different, he seemed different, and the local tabloids made it seem that Philipe was making a bold statement to put uptown down, as though delivering a message. He had showed too much, but people had no idea what was going on in his battered mind and heart. Everyone thought it was a stunt to mock Rainor and uptown, based on the alleged conflict from the tabloids. No one knew anything about a secret love letter to Sally.

Everything in Old Harbor became so rank and file in his perception, like something had suddenly changed; really it was him, it was his manifest destiny. He wasn't sure what he would say to scare Rainor to death, but he knew he would have to put things in order.

Rainor had tapped out from quiet living standards. The same people who were putting him on a pedestal, were now muddying his reputation. Rainor's life was becoming unbearable, and he had no choice but to rectify what Philipe had put upon him with his poison.

First thing the next morning Rainor jumped in his black Mercedes Benz, dressed to kill. Speeding furiously, he was on a mission for retribution.

Rainor met his compatriot, Néné, at the gun store, his aura and presence could be felt right away. "How are you doing my good man?" Néné asked, however futile. Rainor simply shot him a look. Searching for his weapon of choice, he replied, "Not well..." A short pause; instantly, he found what he was looking for. Focusing on his weapon of choice, he said, "Now well." Instinctively, Néné replied, "Understood." He ducked down to carefully take out the gun, bringing it to Rainor's view on top of the counter. "How is this one?" "Well. If you're surefooted and strong in your faith, you will find this black weapon to be your companion, it'll protect you through the thick... But if you're drama is shallow, well you will be destroyed, so please do yourself the favor—." Néné tried to withdraw the gun unsuccessfully, Rainor quickly grabbed a hold of it. "Did you hear what that fake bastard said about me?" "Yes, I read." Néné replied. "You read it?!" Rainor began to flirt with the gun. "That gushy toad, I'll aim for his throat as his maker; no one will hear him croak then." Néné snatched the gun out of Rainor's hands. "Very well," Néné said. "You need to settle down."

"The poor man is going to need more than a prayer." Rainor said, obviously out of his wits. Néné studied him carefully. "Are you sure you don't need help? Anything? For a favor...?"

"None other than this steel." He replied, actioning the hammer.

"Rest assured, good man, but only if you are truly sure, and only if you are surely true."

"That I know I am; pray that I remain that so..."

"So be it." Néné concluded, he loaded the gun with an ammo clip, ad placed it in Rainor's hands carefully, "You're welcome to take these upon you, though I'm warning you; this cannot come back to me."

"I understand..."

"Are you sure?" Néné asked again.

"I am."

A momentary pause, as Néné checked Rainor's resolve. This was the most critical time of their relationship, either Rainor was going to die, kill someone, and bring trouble to Néné at the gun store, or they would be resolved by the faith placed in a greater power.

"I am." Rainor assured him again.

"Good. Then with godspeed, go."

Nothing more was said. As Rainor fled the store blitzing past passers-by in the parking lot, he jumped back into his Benz, hardly giving off any of his heat. He sped away, pushing the gas to the floor, making sure he got where he needed to be fast enough. Nearing the wine estates, his emotions were at an all-time high. The grapevines somehow were eating his soul, its beauty, its natural place in Old Harbor, it was killing him softly. The permanence of wine country was all Rainor could see as he premeditated what he would say to freeze Philipe's blood.

Philipe paced back and forth in his all-too-spacy home now. He was troubled to say the least, mostly broken thoughts and emptiness. He unsheathed his shooter, set it aside, put it in his vest pocket, and pace some more. He was an utter mess, the level of someone meeting ill fate. He looked at himself in the mirror, his mind was playing tricks on him, part vanity, part fear. He continued to unsheathe his gun, loading it and unloading it. "Where is she now?!" He screamed. "Where? Where is my girlfriend?!" The sound of a car's engine, penetrated the estate, it was too close, and, yet getting closer. Looking outside, he noticed Rainor's black Mercedes at the front gate, but no one in it. This was it, his mind was completely gone now, someone was going to get it now. Reloading his gun, he balked and huffed, trapped in space, ready to kill on the slightest pretense. Rainor climbed over a back wall of the gates, sneaking his way into an open window of the mansion.

Furiously, Philipe was speaking his mind, subconsciously warding off the demon penetrating the estate, he couldn't make out who it was. He never saw Rainor make his entrance from the back wall, he crept up, close enough to tackle him, but Philipe was still lost in his own fury to sense a thing. Getting right behind him, Rainor pistol whipped Philipe in the back of the head. "Ow!" Philipe screamed, he fell to the ground, Rainor could have forced him in submission in this very moment, but didn't. As Philipe recovered, he bounced off the ground like a cat. Instinctively, he pulled his weapon and aimed it at Rainor.

51

"Why'd you do it?" Rainor asked hopelessly. Philipe breathing harder now, nearly panting, replied forcefully, "What are you talking about? What are you doing here?! You're the one doing me wrong." "You sold me out. For a story... why? Rainor replied, "You brandished me where my crest had already been ripped out. Rainor continued.

"You have the nerve to come here in your family name with your sins committed against me?" Philipe yelled. "I should end you right now, after you and my girlfriend..." Philipe shouted. "Make your last wish, that your family's legacy still dies with honor."

"You conspire against me, out of your wrath for who, for me? You've been led astray by your own, the ones rowing seeds of evil." Rainor replied.

"Silence!" Philipe shouted, he was becoming out of control. "You cheat with my girlfriend, behind my back, in my own bed, and now wish to humiliate me? You're lucky I don't end this now!"

"What are you speaking of? I was with her, the one night... after that we never spoke. That was it."

"Don't mock me!" Philipe pulled the hammer on his fully loaded gun. Rainor crept out of his skin, for a second he saw his soul leave his body, if he died now he would remain a ghost forever. "Christ, save me, I never touched your girlfriend, I swear to you!" Philipe pointed the nine-millimeter pistol closer to Rainor's head in fury. "Don't lie to me, I saw your letters." "What letters?! Goddamnit there are no letters, I hardly ever touched her, I swear to you—." "Hardly? Stop lying!" He pointed to the walls and fired shots erratically. Rainor pleaded. "I'm begging you Philipe, please, spare my life, my only aim was to set the record straight."

But Philipe continued. "You charge me with callow fear, with spite. I will set you straight." Pausing for a moment, Rainor tried to understand what was going on that Philipe was at the brink of homicide, this muddied in thought and emotion. Philipe shook the gun at his face. "Why?!" He screamed, then he pointed the gun to his own temple. Rainor had lost his cool and pleaded with him frantically, "Please, for god's sake, hold your fire." Philipe came down for a glimpse, caught up in the heat of the moment. "Your pretty friend, Petit, or whatever bad herb, has rooted your mind. Nothing you're saying is even true. None of it. Trust me, Philipe, I'm begging you. Listen to your own good reason. Would I lie to you in my family's name and indignation?" "I saw your letters." Philipe snapped. "Petit told me it was from you."

52

"He lied to you, Philipe. Petit lied. He's a liar and a cheat! Don't you understand?" Philipe reflected for a second, still charged with emotions. Rainor unveiled his weapon. Their emotions were getting the best of them, Philipe shuddered as Rainor pulled the gun from underneath his jacket. 'Why was Rainor even here?' Philipe thought. He was so caught up. "So, what did you plan to do? You came with a gun…"

"I can't live here anymore; my character has been defamed. There's constant curses in my ear. My world is collapsing, it has come down to just you and me, and this needs to end. Nothing you're accusing me of is even true, nor do I wish to conspire against you, as you do to me."

"What are you talking about?" Philipe asked.

"Your story… Why did you do it?" "Story? What story… that gossip column?!" That was a nonsense interview, out of context completely. He practically changed colors in rage. "Take your issue to somebody else. I was never involved with that." Before finishing his sentence, the piercing sound of a police siren blared in the distance. The cops were on their way for them. And in that moment, truth struck Philipe like lightning. "My god, our strings have been pulled… this entire fiasco…" Philipe looked outside helplessly, recollecting his vapid life in its entirety. "The hallow tides of this sad town… we've been washed ashore. No rhyme or reason, just our shallow vanity, our treacherous vanity…"

Gun for gun, bullet for bullet; this was the end of their rope. The sound of blaring sirens was getting louder as police were on their way. Philipe softly admonished Rainor to come closer. They took solace in one another in this moment. Their charges against each other had finally been sorted out; but, perhaps, too late. Philipe touched Rainor's face, and said confidently, "It's plain to see; we were made in the same image… yours black as the dark of night." A surprisingly sanguine look appeared on Rainor's face, he responded, "And you, my counterpart… the light of day." Philipe laid down his silver ,9mm gun. "Show me your arms." Rainor pulled out the black gun from his waist belt, and placed it in Philipe's hands. They were in a numb state of reverie as the sirens grew louder. Philipe gripped the pistol, oblivious to what just took place, this calmed him, like an opiate. He examined the gun, noticing an emblem of the cross Moline brandished on it. Pointing to the cross he whispered, "This, your guiding light… and my silver shooter… doubtless…"

Rainor's reaction was one of solidarity, he wished to die, but he was no longer feeling the need to crawl out of his skin anymore. He looked at the gun sitting

53

on the table. "Go ahead, hold it." Philipe said. Rainor instinctively grabbed the weapon. They looked each other in the eye, no more emotions or verbal assaults. They autonomously leveled their aim at each other's head, almost smiling, as though playing with toy guns. They cocked their pistols in unison, it was an epiphany, the end had come. Philipe whispered, "I always did see myself in you Rainor." Gulping hard and breathing his last breath, Rainor responded, "As did I in you." They opened fire simultaneously, shooting each other in the head at point blank. After the gunshots, they collapsed to the floor, instantly decapitated. Their bodies lied on the floor, motionless, their heads bleeded profusely...

By the time the police arrived, it was too late, both Philipe and Rainor were dead.

The police set up barricades at the scene of the incident, initially deemed a murder suicide, since they had found the letter to be a motive. They said it was a crime of passion, and retribution, an outburst of rage.

After hearing the news over the phone, Sally was devastated. She was in complete shock. When she was questioned about the love letter, she did not have any answers, it was a mystery, even to her.

And when Gia later discovered that Rainor had been shot and killed, she was also deeply saddened, but became extremely frightened for her own safety. This was yet another loss in her life, and she would have to dodge another bullet in her life.

Keith was saddened and perplexed when he heard the news about what had happened. He was convinced it was a murder suicide by Philipe. The police report only revealed erratic gun shots and a quarrel over a love letter. Keith suspected it could have been Petit's fault when he heard about this piece of evidence. He was at the Chateau the night it was written. But he wasn't sure that was it. It was all too shrouded in some mystery for him to wrap his head around it. It seared his mind.

He couldn't stop thinking about his tattoo, the religious inspiration for it, and the double-headed dragon. In his understanding, gospel spoke of a two-headed monster seeking to destroy itself. A two-faced demon, as he understood it. In his life, everything had two sides, the good and the bad, the light and the dark. This crime scene had two guns, one silver, one black, and two people, both decapitated from head

54

wounds. Keith naturally was suspicious that the only motive found was the love letter. Homicide was an extremely rare occurrence in the wine estates, if ever.

The investigation would be an on-going one before authorities could get to the bottom of it. What was most curious was the love letter only had Philipe's fingerprints on it, it never traced back to Rainor. This was highly suspicious, since it was the alleged motive for the crime.

After this horrible murder, Keith could barely function, he only went where his agent and publicists told him to go, he wasn't himself anymore, just a trauma victim now.

In the meantime, his little movie, 'Downtown Exile' was in talks for a sequel, with its immediate success and ticket sales. But the harrowing reflections of the movie to the actual events of Old Harbor were extremely worrisome to Keith. Most troubling was 'Downtown Exile's' plot mirroring the events that eventually took place, nearly identically. The tragic fate of his cousin Rainor, and Philipe. There was a similar love interest, the catalyst for the crime. What's more, Keith had to live with the shrouded mystery of being at the Annulet Chateau the night of Petit's writing of the letter, it was enough to drive him mad. He kept recounting his thoughts, desperately trying to decipher fact from fiction, but couldn't come to any conclusions. He was dying on the inside from all the treachery surrounding his life, in stark contrast to the glitzy fame he was now attaining.

'Downtown Exile' was gaining traction nationwide, and Keith was being recognized as the poster child of Old Harbor society, the living Rainor Gregor, but it was illegitimate fame. He couldn't help but to think how much of a counterfeit he was. Moreover, he couldn't escape his personal religion, this worshipping of a clandestine society, he felt he had died and been reborn as Rainor, resurrected with all his delusions from his movie role. But in his sobriety, he knew the truth, and how he would never be able to attain the complete truth. He never would measure up to the code of integrity that Rainor embodied, the Gregor legacy. Keith was merely a player, not a living man of clan legacy. Yet he still was part of the same social circle, as Rainor's cousin.

In the wake of the alleged murder suicide, Keith felt tremendous guilt, he was gleaning fame from it, plus he was experiencing survivor's guilt. 'That love letter… pure treason… it couldn't have been Petit, could it?' He thought, 'Who else could have written it though?'

After getting blitzed drunk to ward off his demons, Keith was compelled to get a new tattoo. His heart and mind were on fire, a single thought was searing through him, in desperate need of the painful release. A tattoo needle searing into him, he got two tattoos, one was the lettering of 'Loyalty & Betrayal' in Old English typeface; the other was the traditional Cross Moline on his left arm, displaying his allegiance to Rainor and the clan.

A thorough CSI investigation of the incident left everyone scratching their heads still after the scene of the crime. Both guns had Philipe's and Rainor's fingerprints, making it hard to know for sure who used which gun. They deemed it a double homicide, linking Rainor's black brandished gun. The motive for Philipe's murder was uncertain; CSI had concluded that Philipe provoked a fight after the armed Rainor went to visit him, concluding that he was the first to shoot his silver pistol with all the erratic gunshot holes in the wall. It was inconclusive evidence, but fit the order of the crime, based on their line of reasoning.

In prepared remarks to the press, authorities said Rainor had shot to defend himself, making sure they would not unduly smear him in crime reports. This was the greatest of all scandals Old Harbor had ever witnessed, especially in the wine estates. Not only was there no murders in the area, the people involved in the case were in good standing in Old Harbor society.

As the smoke cleared, it was time for Famima to leave town as soon as she received her payment for the story she sold to local tabloids. Two lives were lost, a patriarchy had slowly crumbled, and the entire city was riveted by this unthinkable crime. It was off to a greater and bigger conquest for the gypsy fortune teller. Sylver could spend the rest of his pitiful existence alone, or behind bars, for all she cared.

It was with a broken heart, Sally had gone to both funerals, her beloved Philipe's, and later Rainor's, she looked deeply distraught, in mourning, yet still unable to hide her provocative, fresh young face. At the funeral, Rainor's mother shot her a piercing look as if to say, 'You're not innocent in this, no matter your suffering; you're still the cause of all this.' As it stood, the love letter to Sally was the only piece of evidence for a cause or motive for the crime. Naturally, the women in the Gregor family had nothing but bottled up hatred for Sally.

That same weekend, the LeBlanc family and the entire French conglomerate were forced to dump their entire stock of wine that had gone past its prime, in accordance with protestors and industry regulators who finally caught up to them. Nearly ten million dollars of bad wine had been poured down the Old Harbor river, creating a gushing red tide that flooded all the way to sea.

♣ ♣ ♣ ♣

Limerick Boulevard

"Looking forward to dinner... I'm here. Already... In case you're wondering... Want to see you, tried calling, hope everything's alright. Call me." That was the end of J's voicemail. He hung up the phone. He was alone, left to his own devices, his thoughts began racing... 'I wonder if I should have just kept it at a minimum. We haven't met yet, after all. Should I go? Does she know who I am? Did my reputation scare her off?' His eyes darted around the room searching for familiar faces; but nothing... 'Who am I kidding; I'm just a small fish in a big pond here.'

The sound of roaring engines, and the hustle of warm bodies stirred him up. People at storefronts, taking pictures on the wide and fast Limerick Boulevard. Valet runners and chauffeurs, blinding lights of swanky restaurants and hotels. Later in the night was the last remnants of hope in failed relationships, the surreal dizziness of debutantes, the clashing of cultures and flashing lights, a hint of mortality and the taste of blood in a fight.

One couple attracted attention on the street like a train wreck that night. A young woman was clutching onto her boyfriend's blazer, "Hold me," She cried. "You never hold me, you're always running from me..." They nearly slipped in vomit as her boyfriend carried her off her heels and into his arms.

J just stood there in front of the pub smoking a cigarette, thinking how bad these two had it for love that they would make such a spectacle of themselves. They spoke rapidly and impassioned. Seeing them shouting at each other too obviously and profanely made them loathsome to J. 'How could you do that to yourself?' He thought, 'Why would anyone be that? —' As soon as J could finish his last thought, a black sports car raced up the street, consuming him with the low rumbling of some roaring engine. He saw the car racing up the street and there in the passenger seat was a perfect visual of the girl of his dreams, like it was the first time he had ever seen a girl. Her name was Mellodia, but he didn't know that, she was a rock glam girl that he had seen a couple times before, once on Limerick Boulevard, and the other time in his dreams.

The boulevard spoke to J, so much so, that he could never fail it, nor could it fail him. Earlier in the day, he had risen for another day of celebration. He was a charming, young man, talented too. His success came from his understanding, who he was and what he wanted. There was nothing he did that wasn't for one end in mind: getting the girl. That was the one thing that was indelible to J, above all… because he worshipped women.

He was obsessed with the way they walked, talked, and acted—with all their different mannerisms. He was shamelessly subject to their catty ways, because he was convinced of his own charm. Their skirts, high heels, whether they wore make-up— and how much— it all told a story of the type of woman he was dealing with. Like an animal tamer, he was master and subject to them.

Of course, he had other ends, one of them was confiding in good drink and conversation. Although he didn't hang around much at bars, he would commonly have a drink with his good drinking mate, Jedd. They weren't drunkards, but could steady drink, and normally did until they couldn't form words. At the end of the day, life had no meaning unless they could tell tales. This was a ceremony of storytelling, it relied on trust, the gift of gab, and an immeasurable amount of liquor.

Although J wasn't from the city or the country, he enjoyed where he was, he had rugged good looks that made him wanted by a few girls. For now, he was happy swinging from vine to vine, and pub to pub. He had an interesting job that entailed dealing with talent as a manager and agent, it afforded him a nice social life, to say the least. His day job entailed dealing with new and acclaimed authors at a major publishing house and afforded him a decent social life.

In his spare time, J played music, the guitar was his instrument of choice. From the cello, bass guitar, to drums, J could play a song or two. And he was known for being a damn good amateur, a hobbyist, as well as a lyricist, but he had the voice of a frog, which kept him from ever pursuing music.

He had saved his guitar playing for serenading the ladies, and wrote music in his spare time. But the lyrics he never wrote, it came from the heart. He sang to make his girlfriends laugh. It was never a serious thing, he knew how to make them ooze all over, anyways.

All his time spent on Limerick Boulevard was an inspiration to him. The rhythm of the street was refreshing. He had experienced love in all ways and angles, but he was repressed in ways. As a 30-something year-old without the drop-dead good looks and riches as some of his cohort, J understood that he would have to settle for life in the median someday. He was not opposed to becoming a family man. He had a family that he loved and adored. But he loved living an alternative lifestyle, one abundant in romance and fantasy. What he was lacking was the fulfillment of lovemaking, the type of intimacy that could remind him of his childhood, something that would help him rear children… so he thought. As reasonable as he was, he was also a party animal. Every day was an end. At some point it was only necessary that he had to start anew. But life would start and end with one girl for J, one girl at a time…

The breathtaking and young Mellodia, an erratic beauty, was an enigma of sorts. It was curious how she looked and acted, something of a mute. Yet she overpowered herself in how earnest she was in everything. She was fresh and mesmerizing, just like a young debutante ought to be. She was younger than J, and lived life to the fullest without any regrets, and no end in sight. Mellodia worked with musical groups of all kinds. She fancied rock stars, but one held the keys to her heart, the lead singer of her band that she had started out with. She managed and toured with them, all the way to the States, where she fell in love—not with the lead singer, but with the U.S.

Her American dream was to marry a rock star and live like rock royalty. Although she wasn't there, she had the kind of spunk that any rock star would like, especially Billy. Lead singer of a well-known rock-n-roll group, he was in multiple bands, and had made a name for himself in the rock scene, but around town he was plain old Billy.

Mellodia was touring with a punk rock band called "No-One-And-Done" with a lead singer named Jimmy, who was an edgy son-of-a-gun, but he knew how to flirt with girls, if nothing else. He was the kind of hyper-active thrill seeker that could keep them excited; but, romantically, he was more of a wild boar than a true stallion. Truth be told, Jimmy and Mellodia were too much alike, like two talking heads on a radio show. Mellodia needed to make a name for herself, and he needed to get his rocks off. Fortunately, for her, she had a great vision of nowness, that's to say she lived in the present, was well-traveled and seasoned with road-showing, she had the right stuff to make it in the fame game, but she didn't have a lot of money. Working as a young music professional, she was yet to be loved in the way to become somebody.

The boulevard provided Mellodia everything she needed; music venues, studios, pubs, boutiques, fitness clubs and like-minded people. For someone who didn't have much of an education, she was as brilliant as she looked, and a wild child who came across as shy, but was unafraid to try anything.

Music was her heart and passion; it was a liberating escape, her means to an end. She mostly worked with rock-n-roll bands, but also came across jazz, blues, alternative bands and hip-hop groups. She loved all forms of music, actually.

The band "No-One-And-Done" was playing a punk rock concert a couple blocks up from where J was supposed to have a date. It was raining like hell, the band was known to hold nothing back in their shows and had cultivated a loyal following; punk rock hopefuls, exploited by the system. The world had left them ravaged, giving them more fire to put in their rebellion.

From the stage the singer screamed on the top of his lungs, "How's everyone doing tonight?!" The response was a thunder of screaming fans. "You know I god-damn love you guys! This next song is about the music business, and all those monkeys in suits who don't know what true punk rock is. So here you go..."

◊ ◊ ◊ ◊

J patiently waited for his date with way too much time to think. He sipped his wine with a clear conscious. Although he was by no means a bad person, he was questionable in his interior life. As long as everything was well and good at the end of the day, he was happy.

His date had finally showed, nearly an hour late... a few minutes into the conversation, she already seemed bored and uninterested. Apparently, she was not going to get in the groove of his female submission service. "So, what do you do?" He asked, which led to a five-minute monologue about work, hardship, family, and everything else that was not leading to his one goal in life.

He put up with his stressful job as a literary agent, so he could deal with personalities, this of course afforded him a nice penthouse and a social lifestyle. Like most guys, J wasn't concerned with having fancy toys, personal possessions, investments, or cars—unless they helped him get the girl. Life was simple in J's eyes; his penthouse, a love motel; his car, a way to his penthouse; his girlfriend: the end.

It was the end game J had trouble with, everything else could sustain itself; but J worshipped women, so much so, you could say it was an addiction. That meant he was stuck up in the clouds with romance and intimacy. Like any addiction, it was predestined to kill him, one way or another, but he didn't mind. He would die without it, a worse way, or not at all. His biggest fear was becoming topsoil without ever living out his life.

He didn't look like the kind of bloke to put pussy on a pedestal, but he was. He was that person; and as far as the eye could see, he might have been the only one.

Inevitably, J's date came up with an excuse, supposedly she had to take care of her sister that night, and she abruptly left J alone before even ordering. That was a first for him. If he ever got stood up, it was a no-show, or the girl would just ignore him after he bought her a second or third drink.

Luckily, his waitress was sympathetic, shy wasn't shy to spend a minute at his table showing off her breasts. She insisted J order a meal, giving him another glass of white wine.

Everyone in that warm place was happy and buzzing along. Waiting for his meal, J got a little self-conscious; he worried he had permanently lost his touch and sterling charm. He was vulnerable and exposed now, all alone.

After eating by himself, J left on foot for the nearest pub. He had a heavy mind, thinking and overanalyzing why his date left so early. His identity was his ability to get girls—his charm, his saucy drinking antics. This was hard to swallow for him, he was now alone and rejected. But J just walked it off as he headed for the nearby bar.

There, in the dark pub, his eyes glowed as he stepped inside. His need for intimacy was shooting through the roof, after being let down on his date. He not only needed a woman fast, he needed the holy grail of life… he needed sex.

◊ ◊ ◊ ◊

After the show, Mellodia joined up with "No-One-And-Done," they were spent, now wasting away in a green room. One of them was petting a fawning groupie. Melli handed them a huge wad of cash full of $20's. The lead singer, Jimmy, just looked at her and asked, "What is this?"

— "He won't take the money."

— "What do you mean?"

— "He wants me to go on tour with the band."

— "So, we're not going to jam?"

— "You're just going to have to wait, he's not willing to do anything yet."

— "Get him willing to do something then!"

She gave him a cross look. "So, what are you doing tonight?" She asked. "Going out... partying...you coming?"

"I think I'm gonna walk." "No, don't walk, c'mon, we'll give you a lift at least."

— "I'll be fine."

— "You sure?"

— "Yes, I'm sure." She replied.

— "Okay, then... so long."

— "See ya."

— "Walk on M!" Another band mate blurted out.

She left the back of the club and made her way through an alleyway to the main boulevard. On her way home was a major pub where J had landed earlier.

J had four empty shot glasses in front of him with his mate as he shot back his last drop of whiskey.

"One more, one more!" "No, I'm done, thanks." J replied. "Cheers, anyway." "Ya, cheers... to you, and youth." "I'd rhyme all day, if I could too!" They slammed their shot glasses down. "One more?!" "No, really I can't." "Ahaha, yes you can, you little bastard you!" J eventually conceded. And so, they forced down another shot of the hard.

Stepping outside to light a smoke, J noticed someone walking up the street, as if the world had just stopped, it was none other than Mellodia. She brushed up against him like a cat warming up to be petted. J threw away his cigarette and began his chase. "Hey, don't I know you?" She glanced at him quickly and put her nose in the air. "You're that rock glam girl. You were here earlier. Yeah, I've definitely seen you!"

She kept walking down the boulevard, hardly noticing him. "What are you doing running from me?" She paused looking at him, curiously, as if to say, 'Well, aren't you going to do something about it?' "Don't you know that every guy you pass like that is thinking the same thing? Huh, you know that?" Still a cold shoulder... J scooted up and grabbed her arm. She looked alarmed, but unafraid. "I just wanted to ask, what are you doing here all alone?" "I've got to get home." She replied. "Going home? This early? C'mon let me give you a lift, the least I can do...c'mon." But she didn't budge, she just stood there in front of him like the world was going to end. "You're going to give me a ride?" "Yes, of course, I can give you a lift..." He answered. "Fine then. I'll wait here." "Okay... Okay, hold on for me. I'm J by the way, J. Willemson..."

"That's nice." She replied apathetically.

"How about you?"

"What?"

"Your name...?"

As if she wasn't going to tell him her name, he waited for her jaw to move miraculously, to tell him. "Mellodia, my name's Mellodia." He smiled at her like he had just won the lottery. "Mellodia... now that's a pretty name...!" He had a hunch she was going to escape him if he didn't hurry, he pulled out his phone. "Say Melli, I don't think I have your number yet." She just stood there, caught completely off guard. You want to give me your number?" "What for?" She snapped back. "Well, so I could give you a call, and we could go out sometime." "I might not have any time for that... If you're going to take me to my house, I can give it to you later."

"So, you want to give me your number later? Give me the last four digits, I'll bet I can guess it." She started to rattle off her number with abandon. As if pulling the numbers from thin air, he memorized it right away. "Got it, great! I'll give you a call sometime then! How's that sound?" No reply, just a pleasant. "Alright, so you'll wait for me here?" "Yes, hurry up."

He rushed to his car, and started it up for what seemed like ten minutes. He had a great feeling he was going to lose the chase, the way she was pounding up the boulevard. As he drove up to where she had been standing, he didn't see her anywhere in sight. She vanished. But he had her number memorized; not knowing for sure if that was her proper number.

J barely slept that night, he was so obsessed with the girl that he wanted to call, despite knowing that he should wait a couple days without coming across too desperate. She was an "It" girl though. He tossed and turned thinking and re-thinking, all the countless ways he could have finagled his way to her house that night or at least gotten to second base in his car. 'Didn't she know he drove a fancy sports car. Didn't she care?' He thought. On one hand, she could care less about him, on the other hand, they had just met for the first time, and J was coming on strong without any real block or defense from her. Still, he couldn't help but to think negatively with his hand itching to dial that one number that could unlock everything good in his life. He hadn't gone on one date with the girl and already he had professed his love for her and had her number memorized.

The phone was buzzing, the ringtone played a rock ballad on Mellodia's cell. "Yes?" She answered. It was Billy. "I want a second chance," he said. "I know how you want me to record with your band in the studio. And I'm willing to do it, to do anything… if you promise you'll go on tour with us, with me."

— "Okay…"

— "So, is that a 'yes'?"

— "If you agree to record with the band."

— "Absolutely! What are you doing this weekend?"

— "I'd rather wait 'til you're with the band." She said.

— "It'd have to be sometime before the weekend. We've got a show and then we go on tour."

— "Alright, why don't we set something up for this Thursday. I'll be with them then."

— "Fine, fine." He replied, "Will I see you on the weekend at least?"

— "Yeah, no problem."

◊ ◊ ◊ ◊

"God, how great could one love be?" J nudged Jedd, "If I was with her, and she loved me, too. To think that I, J. Willemson, could actually be loved by a woman, and equally love that woman at the same time!"

"You need a kick in the head…? You need to get a vasectomy, before you wreak havoc on this place…"

"Ha-Ha… the point is, I'm in love." His eyes shimmered in truth, intoxicating truth. "Ya?" "Yes, am… there isn't a moment that goes by that I don't think about it." J proclaimed. "Well, then what are you doing talking to me?"

"I haven't quite met her yet—" J replied.

"Come again?" Jedd was perplexed.

"—Besides, you should know you never call a girl as soon as you've met her.

A group of women walked into the bar, one older, and strikingly beautiful, she grabbed Jedd's attention as the younger gal—a flower in her hair—went to order a drink at the bar. Jedd had his eyes fixed on her, she looked back, obviously attracted.

"I'm confused, you haven't met'r?" "That's right." "What is she, some kind of star?" "She's in music. Let me just give you an idea of what I'm talking about, what I mean about calling a girl."

"You see that girl over there, with her friends, the one that left the table right there?" "Which girl, the girl with the flower in her hair?" "Yes, you haven't noticed her?" "Of course," "I'm sitting opposite of you and I noticed her as soon as she walked in." "So, what are ya saying? That you got extra peripheral vision?"

65

"Just watch." Jedd was taken by J's confidence as he snapped a one-eighty and approached this young, beautiful girl. 'This is the stuff youthful charm was made of.' Jedd thought.

For a man to be made in this scene he had to make conversation no matter what. It was chat, and chat some more, or fail miserably.

All the pride and glory of Jedd's wild youth was playing out before him in a couple lasting moments. From his point of view, he saw all the right moves, he reminisced to when he was in his prime, the way a guy talked to a gal and kept talking: near her ear and away from her eyes. And when you winked at someone, it meant something. He looked over at the older gals now standing at the bar, he didn't dare wink at them, just glanced at their shiny globes, taking in the scene from J who could have talked for days with this girl, she was laughing and happy as can be. But J still hadn't proved anything to him yet, no matter the marvel.

As he walked back like a million bucks, Jedd asked him, pregnant with curiosity. "So, what'd you tell her?"

"Everything and nothing…"

"That wasn't nothing. She was hanging on your every word. What'd you say?"

"I shared a lyric of a song with her, she got a kick out of it. That's it…"

"So, is this the girl you're in love with?" J chuckled and pounded his beer down. "Is it?" Jedd asked again. J just nodded his head. "Can't you see, I must have spoken with her for nearly five minutes, and sure we like each other… but a girl that's in love melts in your arms, she gushes her panties, whispering sweet blessings and moaning blasphemies, what else is there to do than carry her away and give her the loving she needs?"

"You still haven't said anything." The girl and her friends now headed for the exit.

J pulled out a handkerchief with a name and number written on it in perfect girly penmanship and handed it to him. "What's this?" Jedd asked. "Her mam's number, she's got an eye for you. And she says if you don't call her soon she's never coming back to this shitty dump again." The girl's mom turned around and gave Jedd

66

a saucy wink. Jedd laughed incredulously. "Alright… alright!" Jedd sprung to his feet. "So, you going to call her?" Jedd shouted at the girl's mom, fair warning that he would give chase, and bolted towards her before she left.

◊ ◊ ◊ ◊

In a narrow alleyway was Billy's private studio. It didn't seem like much from the outside, it didn't look like a studio at all from the outside. Inside it was pitch black.

Mel and her band had come to record after their show. Standing at the door, Billy hit the lights. It was a perfectly well-kept place. "Very nice studio!" "Thanks." It was remarkably clean and well-lit, all the equipment was perfectly kept, not one speck of dust, at all. There were hallmarks of rock star originality with mixed media patriotic paintings and tattoo art on the wall. Traces of notable bands that recorded there lined the wall with award plaques. Billy flipped another switch to turn on a hologram of Elvis Presley. "Wow!" Jimmy said in amazement.

"You've got a hologram of Elvis?!" Billy chuckled, "Ya." "That's incredible!" Jimmy replied.

"So, you wanna show me what you got?" Billy demanded. "Okay, ya…" He began strumming on the guitar, "We kind of want it to sound like this…" Jimmy plucked the strings for a few power chords. "But better…"

"Kinda like this?" Billy played a couple beats on the soundboard and strummed the electric guitar.

"Yeah, that! That sounds great!"

"Okay! Yeah, I can definitely get this rolling." Billy cried out.

The rest of the band showed up not too long after. It only took them a few hours to mix. Later in the evening, Billy gave Mellodia a call to get down to the studio by herself. The band was happy with the mixing session, and so was she, so she had no problem going on Billy's request. He delivered what she wanted, and finally, he was going to get what he wanted.

When she arrived, Billy brushed his nose against her neck, no sooner than she could say anything. She surrendered to him and accepted his loving. He smelled so good to her. She always thought he was nice and charming, just didn't want him to fall in love with her. He began to taste her neck, her lips, and moved in to un-strap her bra after she flung her top off. Her skin was creamy and supple; she smelled like honeydew from her body lotion. Billy attacked her lips, uncontrollably possessed by her wild, unbridled and freakish beauty. He grabbed her by the waist and sat her down on a flat table to rip her jeans off; her cell phone fell to the floor. Billy started undoing her panties, the phone buzzed on. It was J calling—a inopportune time to call. "Hello, Melli?" He shouted in the phone. But she couldn't hear him, the phone just lit up on the floor. "Hello, are you there?" His voice rang out, anxiously. The faint panting of Melli began to creep into the receiver. J didn't hang up, but listened helplessly, Mel started panting harder and harder. Billy thrust himself on to her, there was nothing J could do but listen to them having sex. It was guttural and predictable, a lot of grunts, moans, and a lead up to fireworks with all the usual profanities.

J wasn't sure if this was intentional, but it was an emotional thrill ride for him; first fear, then despair, excitement, and finally, jealousy. 'Who was this guy who was able to make her scream out loud? And why was I listening in to this?' J was beginning to think there was more to Melli than what met the eye. He knew now she wasn't the prude she made herself out to be, she lived up to her sexy, wild looks with this.

Billy finally laid off. She got back up from the table where she had been pinned in romance. Her clothes were thrown all over the floor along with Billy's. She looked up at him as he was putting on his jeans back on, somewhat pathetically.

— "That was amazing." She gasped.

— "Yes. It was." Billy had already come down, he seemed almost embarrassed at this point. It was all for the sex really, there was no questioning their rapport.

— "What do you got going on now?"

— "Just work, basically."

— "Make a song for me, ya?" She asked.

— "Make you a song? You mean write you a song?" He asked.

— "It's not too much trouble?"

68

— "No…not at all… like right now?"

— "Yes. Right now,"

— "Sure, I'll play a song for you…"

— "But I want you to play it for me."

— "Okay" He threw on his shirt, grabbed his acoustic guitar and started stringing chords together to belt out a tune.

"Melli… oh Melli… you are; the apple in my pie…. And I know it's true… no other girl I'd rather swoon, but you… you're the apple in my pie, the apple in my pie, the apple in my pieeee…"

She started to giggle at his ballad. "Not bad…" She responded, giving him a dainty clap.

"Not bad? That was freaking great." He said jokingly. "So, what do you got going on now?"

"Oh, nothing much. You're taking me home, ya?"

"Yeah, as in my home…"

He slapped her on the thigh still kidding around, but she got a little shy. She let out a little giggle to keep the mood light, but she was still a little intimidated by him.

"C'mon, let's get your little sexy ass out of here!"

As they left, Mel checked her phone, noticing the missed calls. J had called her a second time, that was two missed calls. She had no idea that he had overheard her having sex.

J was made to feel the same emotions and basic instincts. Fighting this off, he had gone back to meet with Jedd; same boulevard, different pub.

69

Jedd cajoled him, "What's going on with you J, how ya doing?" "Troubled. I called the girl, but no answer…" He replied.

"Got to be patient, ya always got to be patient with women."

"Yeah, I don't know…"

"Have another shot." Jedd pushed a shot glass in front of J. They both downed it in unison like synchronized swimmers. Just then a pack of women entered. "Well, look at what just came through the door." The girls were giddy, traipsing their way to the bar, just another girls' night out for them.

J noticed one of them; at first glance, he thought she looked just like Melli. It got him excited. Immediately, he was fixing on what he was going to say to them. The one girl he had his eye on, Melli's doppleganger, had long blonde hair and a healthy supple body for such a petite girl. After they ordered a drink, J approached her.

—"Hi there."

—"Hi…" The girl replied.

— "What's your name?"

— "Me?" She asked.

— "Yes, you, what's your name?

— "Melanie."

— "Oh, that's purrty. You come here often?"

— "Sometimes, why?"

— "No, I just never seen you here before."

He extended his arm, "I'm J." He said, giving her a firm handshake. When she shook hands, he took her palm and kissed it.

She giggled. "You're too cute…"

"Oh yea?" J replied, "What makes you say that?"

70

"I don't know, you just are..."

He smiled at her, "I'm at that table over there, if you want to join us..." He pointed over to Jedd, "How about I buy your next round?"

"Thanks, but I'm going to stick tight... girl's night out and all." A change in expression fell on J's face.

"Sure thing," He replied.

She turned around and looked at him with an inviting smile as she left the bar. J was slightly shook up, but not defeated. J just pounced on the next woman to walk in like a cat after his prey. He had learned in his early years of clubbing and bar hopping that to get a girl you had to be constantly going at it and leave once you've got what you wanted. Sometimes he got a number, sometimes a fake number, and sometimes the girl. He always knew the fake numbers by the way the girl handled the exchange. Every time it was a curious question, out of fear, a glance, or hesitation.

J was determined to get Melanie's number. So, he attacked the next couple of girls with vengeance, grabbing one of the girls by the waist as he brushed past her, hoping to make Melanie smitten by him. He looked back to see if she was sneaking a peak. She was. That was a good sign. When a girl looked back to sneak a peek, it meant she was interested, and he had a one-hundred percent success rate with girls who showed interest in him.

Witnessing J's playful come-on, a young guy straggling behind the girl stared right at him without any real emotion.

"You like that? Not bad huh?" J said to the straggler.

"Well, yeah. Actually, that's my girl... so no, I don't like that."

"Oh, I had no idea..."

He had to dodge a confrontation and make his way back to his table. Jedd's seat was empty now, he was having a cigarette outside. Sitting alone, J kept giving filthy looks to Melanie, who was sitting adjacent to him. She looked back, she was interested.

The other girl, oddly, was nowhere near the straggling gentleman J had bumped into. The straggler claimed to be her boyfriend. 'How could he be her

71

boyfriend? He was nowhere near her.' J thought. At any rate, he sat alone giving lusty looks to the beautiful doppelganger, his infatuation for the night. She left the table to go to the bar. As she was waiting for her drinks, J made a bold move and approached her. They locked eyes for a moment. Standing next to her, drink in hand, he got nearer and asked, "—Ask you a serious question?" He asked. "What is it?" She replied.

"Are you wet right now…?" He searched in her eyes for a confident response. "Sopping." She replied. Maintaining eye contact, he asked, "Do you get wet often?"

'Yes', she nodded. "What's your number?" Without skipping a beat, she wrote it down and handed it to him. J gave it a quick glance, and smiled wide. "I'll give you a call tonight." "Can't, gotta take care of my girls." She smiled back at him. "Okay, when?" "I don't know, whenever…" She replied. After saying his peace, he left the bar alone. That was J's night.

◊ ◊ ◊ ◊

Busy at work, J found a minute to pick up his cell phone, he texted Mellodia. Normally, he wouldn't go through texts and phone calls at work, but he was mad. He was madly in lust with the world, and Mellodia was the cause.

A couple hours went by, still he received no word back from her. It made him curious, 'How could she ignore me when she didn't even know who was calling?' He thought to himself. It would be understandable if she was avoiding him, but she didn't even have his number to know. Another thing that was curious was how her voicemail was a robotic automated voicemail. 'Maybe she just doesn't take any calls at all.'

Thinking about this made J a little distraught, but he still had Melanie's number, and the way she was looking at him the other night made it seem like a for sure thing he was going to get lucky. He called her with the hum drum from work in the background. The only thing on J's mind now was scoring his ace in the hole with Melanie. The phone rang, and rang, and rang. Finally, she picked up. "Hello, Melanie?" "Yes…?" She replied, coquettishly. "Hi Melanie! I was seeing if you wanted to… if you wanted to meet up!"

— "Ooh, I love the sound of that. I was hoping you'd call."

— "Okay, great, well I'm off work at 6:00, so why don't we meet up then?!"

— "Tonight? Well I'm a little bit busy tonight..."

— "Busy? Busy with what?"

— "I gotta wash my hair."

— "Oh ya? Well you can wash it after."

— "I don't know..."

— "C'mon you just said you were glad I called."

— "Yea I know. Not tonight, really, I'm busy."

— "Alright, well you've got my number, I'll text you my address if you change your mind."

— "Okay, good." She replied, then hung up.

Back at his house, J's guitar stared at him, her name was 'Diamond', it was the most beautiful looking guitar he'd ever had, white with sterling strings, it left only minor calluses, a lot more manageable than harsher strings. He picked it up, plucking a couple of chords into his existential loneliness, J found a melody.

"Girl on the backstreets, you're the one I adore, just from our small rapport...

Hey girl, you know that, you're one in my heart.... right from the very start..."

He continued to play in the key of 'C', plugging at the tune, while finding lyrics.

"It's just you and me... but we're lost at sea... for good."

Plucking the strings, and slowly finishing, he had Mellodia in mind. His mind played a scene of how he would make love to her, like a romantic freak of nature, having to blindly feel and always needing more.

J went to the kitchen, in an open abyss of glorious counter tops and hallow spaces, hardly any food, but plenty of drink. He cracked open a bottle of whiskey, his go-to drink. Pouring out the whiskey always gave him a sense of pride, knowing he had bought that bottle with his own money, he bought his car and paid for his apartment with his job. He worked like an indentured servant for it. He was an agent without the same mobility as an executive, but he still had to work to earn his stripes, and it paid well. Spilling his drink from the pour, he reflected on his job and life, all at once. As the whiskey went down, he played with his pretty guitar in his beautiful, empty, space.

◊ ◊ ◊ ◊

Melli was a pin-up doll, toying with her wavy, blonde hair, she stood in front of Billy outside of the club, while the open door let out blaring rock ballads.

— "So, this is it." Billy told her. "We're going on tour after this."

— "I know."

— "Well, what do you say?" Are you going to come with us, or what?"

— "I don't know. You keep asking me, makes me not want to go actually."

— "You know what Melli?" He replied somewhat irritated. "Sometimes I don't know what's going on with you..."

— "Don't get mad." She replied.

— "Listen, girl, you know you're my little rock star princess, so just come."

He flipped her hair like she was a little girl. Normally, she would have flicked a guy away, but rock stars were irresistible to her, 'how could he do that?' she thought. Her mind went aflutter. 'How could he just flip the argument in his favor? Was I not being fierce enough? Is he going to get the best of me? I don't care. I want him. Right now, only now.'

— "I am your rock star princess?" She asked.

Caressing her face, he went in for a kiss, but she pulled away. "Yeah, and I want to tug your hair in a tight pony tail. You're driving me crazy!" He said. He glided his hand through her wavy, gorgeous mess of blonde and brown hair.

◊ ◊ ◊ ◊

74

A stage hand came outside to give Billy the heads-up that they were about to show. "Hey Billy, we need you on stage, you're going on in ten."

A transient caught a glimpse of the shimmering scene, "Hey, you're, Billy-Joe-what's-his-face...!"

Billy froze, literally looking like a pile of stone. He just pretended to be talking to the stage hand. "Your band is the greatest! Rock & Roll for life!"

Billy shot at look at the passerby. "Cheers!" He exclaimed. The passerby maintained his gaze as waltzed off.

"Alright princess, time to go." Melli thought the stagehand was talking to her. She rushed into the club, "No, not you." Billy grabbed her by the arms and smacked a kiss on her lips hard. "Come with us." "Okay." She replied.

She was left in the cold as he went backstage. She stood there a moment, in the club catching a cold as she attempted to step in but the bouncers did not allow her, directing her to another side entrance.

She made her way in, near the stage, her brains getting beat in by an opening band that she didn't particularly care for. She was confused for a moment, so she went outside to the front of the club on the boulevard. Two other straggling hopefuls were sitting near the sidewalk, one was a call girl wearing a leopard-skin coat. Melli pretended to check her phone for messages.

"Hey you..." Melli looked up, instantly she recognized who was talking to her, but had never spoken with her before. "Hi." She replied coyly. "How does it feel being the flavor of the week?" Melli just looked right past her. "Don't think that we haven't been there, darling'. "What? With Billy?" Melli asked. "Yea, you're his little girly, girl right now. "He's my boy toy." She replied smugly. "Oh confident... are you really now? What are you going to do later when he's not with you..."? She took a drag of a cigarette between her lips, squinting at Melli, studying her. "What do you do?" She asked. "What do you mean?" Melli replied. "For work, what do you do? You're always tapping your hot little feet down the boulevard, I wanna know." "I manage 'No-One-And-Done'. And releasing a single with the band, with Billy. The call girl had a skanky look on her face. "Oh yeah? Well, let me tell you something, you might be riding high today, but tomorrow you'll be on the curb like the two of us." Making no eye contact, both the girls wore a scowl on their faces formed from the disgust of being on the streets for too long.

Before they could get any more depressed, a troubadour sounded from a couple blocks away; a guitarist and a marching drummer band. They were hymning a tune on the top of their lungs.

"Oh, sweet dreams, oh lovely sweet thing, let me sweep you off your feet, off this poor, decrepit street.

Oh, sweet lovely thing, you're all alone with a bow in your hair, you know that I care, and I'm here when I'm there, that I'll be there when I'm there... you know that I love but-won't-ever-dare...

Oh, sweet lovely thing, won't you sing when I sing, dream a lovely dream when I dream, make this song ring with a ring..."

The troubadour approached the girls in front of the club, Mel could hear the band go on. She went back in the club. Outside, the guitarist started serenading the two women outside.

"Oh, lovely sweet thing, can't you see? Will you hear my plea? What are we, when it's you... without me? Let me sweep you, sweep you off your feet, let's leave this boulevard, and streets... Oh, sweet thing, here's my plea... for you and for me, let's make it for you and for me..."

They threw a couple white roses at the call girl and her friend, and continued strolling along. "What should we do now?" Her friend asked. "Go to the alley pub. That's where they'll end up anyhow." The call girl replied. "We can meet them there, I'm starving."

◊ ◊ ◊ ◊

J got drunk from all the whiskey at the pub, and now was playing the guitar to his heart's content—alone in his apartment, until a knock on the door woke him out of his lull. The doorbell rang, again, and then once more. He ran to the front door, looking through the peephole, it was Melanie. 'It's her!' He brushed himself off quickly, and carefully opened the door. "I changed my mind." She said. "I can't believe it! So glad you're here, let me get your coat..." He took off her coat and instinctively grabbed her by the hand to walk her inside. "Do you need a drink?" "No, just you." She said.

Laying on the sofa, her eyes searched his, he kneeled and nuzzled his face next to hers and began taking off her clothes. She took off her shirt; he pulled her bra strap down off her shoulder and started to kiss her naked flesh while working on undoing her jeans. He went down to her torso and slowly took off her jeans to reveal her rose and black-laced lingerie, which was already moist. He teased her body, moving his fingers around her waist underneath her panties. Facing opposite her face, he began to massage her feet, which were kept pretty and polished. All he thought at this moment was how he wished he could see her perfect feet curl when they would eventually wrap around his body. Then he turned around. Slowly he stretched and pulled off Melanie's underwear. She had a Brazilian wax, a nice change to what J was used to. Carefully, he straddled her legs on the sofa and began to gently rock and sway, their bodies smashed closely against each other.

J then kneeled in front of Melanie on his knees, rubbing his face against her shapely lower abs. She had the kind of lower body that was fit from having a good amount of sex, all the contortions and straddling had whipped her body in shape.

She bowed her body back as J's tongue searched and sucked her clit in a frenzy, she grabbed her full C-cup breasts and moaned in ecstasy while his tongue slowly worked in and out of her. He kept at this for a while until her body language told him that he had hit the spot, he surprised her by puckering his lips on it, making a smooching sound, a trick he used to keep women titillating in fits and bursts. He tasted her clit, she kept shivering and coming in his mouth. She grabbed his full head of dark brown hair and massaged it, pushing his mouth further into her body, curling her red polished toes. After her orgasmic fit, J figured she had probably come two or three times already; he gave her saddle a tap and stood up. She turned around to do a reverse cowboy, but he shook his head, "Lay down again." She laid down as she was. He got on top of her and began to passionately kiss her. She preferred rugged, but he was in his own world, his face kept tight and remarkably handsome as she stared into his shiny globes. He gave her nothing but filthy glances. All the fantasies of being with a dark horse romancer, a passionate lover, and someone infatuated with her. He fit the bill for her. She just relaxed and let him romance her. Her eyes rolled back and she bit her lip in fits of ecstasy. This was it, the moment he had been waiting for, her 'O' face... and it was a long-lasting one.

◊ ◊ ◊ ◊

The band inside the club was in full swing with their rock-n-roll set, Billy was owning the stage, while Mellodia stood in front of the crowd, it was as if he didn't

77

see her, or she didn't stand out, because he just looked past her. She was lost in a sea of people, and Billy was barely noticing her. After a few songs like this, she couldn't take it anymore, and so she went outside, and called J out of desperation.

The phone buzzed, but he couldn't hear it, it was flung across the room with his slacks. This time she sincerely wished J would sweep her off the street. After another failed attempt to call, she left for home, walking past the alley pub where the call girl and her friend had landed. The troubadour made eye contact with her as she passed by, all alone, burning an image into her memory.

Once she got home, Mellodia kicked of her shoes and socks and went to the freezer to grab a pint of her favorite sorbet ice cream. She was tired of the whole drama of the day. Missing J's calls, hooking up with Billy, feeling let down, and uncertain about going on tour; it all swirled in her head like a brewing storm. She would have to take her work with her, and for how long she could do that was up in the air. She ended up in front of the television, exhausted. She eventually passed out.

◊ ◊ ◊ ◊

Still in missionary position, J flipped his thick brown hair back. He moaned and groaned while Melanie screamed for him to keep going. As he finally came, he screamed out Melli's name. There was nothing Melanie could do but wonder, 'Why is he calling me Melli? He hasn't ever called me Melli.' She thought, 'Oh that feels good, oh ya right there, don't stop, don't stop.' "Don't stop, baby, don't stop." She was shouting now. Eyes shut, he had his orgasm, dreaming of Mellodia. Both of them were panting, coming down from death-defying sex. Melanie crashed on the sofa and rolled over.

J quickly left the room. Just as Melanie was about to pass out, he quickly lit candles in the living room and turned on some music on his stereo surround sound. Melanie was in a neverland, nearly falling asleep as the music played. 'Oh, what nice music', she thought to herself, subconsciously. 'Weird that he listens to this, I wonder if this is what death feels like—oh I love this music though, I love spiritual things, spiritual people, oh yes all those great, grand people, everything can be spiritual really, sex, orgasms, even—well sex some of the time, or all of the time, or most of the time…' As she dozed off in tranquility, J ripped her by the arm and aggressively turned her around, her bare-naked breasts shook like pillows.

78

"J! What are you doing?" He poured hot candle wax on her chest. "Ouch, that's hot!" "Oh ya!" J replied, apathetically. He started rubbing it down her belly and got on his knees. "What are you doing J?" "Shhh" "What the hell is this?!"

"Happiness, and fulfillment..."

Melanie didn't know what to do or say, she was feeling dizzy from all the scents and sounds, and now J was in wide-eyed prayer in front of her naked body. She had never experienced anything quite like this and she could hardly believe it. He began to rub her body with his fingertips putting her at ease. Lifting her leg, he started to massage her feet. Now standing up, he kissed her leg up and down her calf and thigh. She calmed a bit as he continued for another minute. She thought it was outrageous and bizarre, but she couldn't deny she was beginning to like it, like every other outrageous fetish; it was another notch, and a wildly different one...

After they were done, she gave him a courteous kiss and went out the door of his apartment, without any intention of ever seeing him again. J took a shower and passed out on the couch, still envisioning her face.

The next day, J finished reading a new novel submitted to his desk, it read like the thousands of other fantasy fiction stories that had reached his desk. J threw the manuscript in the trash and started jotting down notes on his calendar. 'Same old stuff.' He said to himself, 'If I got a nickel for every time I read a fantasy book with the same plot...' Then he got a text message on his phone, he noticed he had a missed call from Melli, who else? Here was his chance... 'Maybe she turned the corner', he thought.

One of the interns walked into his clear glass office. "What should I tell Howie?" "Pass it down, I don't want to get involved with this." "He's at the front." "Who?" J asked incredulously. "Howie..." "Oh Christ... alright, bring him in then." "One second." The young intern snapped back to the front office and greeted a haggard looking bird-watcher of a writer. Howie, who wore a feather in his cap, literally, was not a happy looking man. As he entered J's office, J chuckled a little greeting him. "Hi Howie, how are you?"

"Shit. That's how I am." He gave him a star-searching gaze as the air left the building for a moment. "Look, I read the manuscript you sent me, and I'll be honest with you, it doesn't sound like one of your original works." Howie looked like he wanted to say something, but J kept fast-talking. "It reads like every other romance fantasy novel I've ever read." Howie reacted agitated and asked, "Isn't that what's selling? I'm trying to write something that will put me back on top." J clenched his face while still attempting to hide his stress. Taking a deep breath, he said, "Howie, now let me be frank, I've known you for a little while. You're one of a kind, I realize that, and a piece of work, I must say, just ask anyone that knows you—no one knows your writing better than I do. But you've got to be yourself, write your own story, a romance fantasy novel that has the storyline of a day-time soap opera plot isn't going to make the cut." "Don't you think, it's a work of literary prowess? Those are the notes I got from a review…"

"Your language is great, don't get me wrong… you're great Howie. You've always been great, but you've essentially wrote the plot to play like 'Days of Our Lives' with a few other twists. Honestly, I like how lyrical you are—maybe write a story with more lyrics or poetry." "What are you telling me? To write a book of poems?" Howie asked, now looking more furious than ever. "No, no, I mean write something musical, that can be adapted for the stage, a Broadway musical, for example…"

"I thought you said you wanted a romance fantasy?"

"I change my mind." J sighed. "I've been getting nothing but the same, you showed me something different last time you were here… I thought this was going to be something more in line with your other novel."

"Jesus J, I've been tossing and turning, gritting my teeth for nothing?! You said you wanted romance-slash-fantasy."

— "I told you… I change my mind. It doesn't pan out."

— "Why romance in the first place? What, do you have some kind of fetish?!"

— "Me? No, of course not, I mean, why would you even think—ha-ha, I don't have any fetish." He retreated a little. "I wouldn't call it that anyhow…"

No response. "Here's the thing: romance fantasy is a big trend; and, initially, I thought the publishers could get behind a few good titles… I mean you're a great writer Howie. You writing something like this makes me think your best romance years are behind you… or ahead… I can't really tell."

80

"Christ, why don't you just tar and feather me while you're at it? Were you waiting for me to fall off the face of the Earth to tell me this, or a fucking roast ceremony?!" He paused for a moment, trying to catch another angry breath. Admit it J, you have some kind of fetish, it's not the end of the world, you can tell me the truth..."

J gave him a look that didn't appease Howie at all. "Let's be open, shall we? I'm dating a woman, fifteen years older than me, and she's got great instincts in literature, mind you. We both have our barnacles, we accept that. It's not always pretty... but we're great together, anyways, we've been having open dialogue about love, life, spirituality, books, everything... and this is the direction I want to go with my writing. Can't you see? It's more sophisticated..." J acquiesced.

"How about you J, what have you done lately in your love life?" "For Chris sakes Howie, let's not get into this..." "You have some fetish angle, I know it." Howie reprimanded. "What is it? You don't have to hide it from me. You can tell me." "Howie, when was the last time you got laid?" "All the time." He replied defensively. "When was the last time you've been on the Boulevard, the Riviera, the Big City? The Boulevard, Howie. When was the last—" "I don't know..." Howie replied. "Last New Year's—not this past New Year's—but the one before that, why?"

"I go to the Boulevard every weekend, sometimes on the weekdays, whenever I get the chance." "And...?" "And I take a new girl to my apartment at least once a week. Don't you understand—?" Howie got upset, interrupting him, "Oh I see... this circus is your little ego booster, you get to pretend to be a big shot-caller so you can belittle lowly writers like myself. Well, let me tell you something J, I'm not just any writer. And you are full of—" J interrupted, "—Don't you understand Howie? What I'm saying is, I've seen all the gags, I've lived out the drama. When I see, the same thing inked on the page, it's already old news, I want to throw it in the bin and wash my hands of it."

"Oh ya?" Howie replied. "And you think I was born yesterday... goddamnit J, you know what happened to me, my last wife, my past life..." "She left you for another... another author."

Agitated, Howie air-punched the wall. "I let her slip through my hands J, she slipped through my hands, like quicksand... I know she still loves me. But I have only myself to blame."

"Look, Howie, you gotta get past all that and move on." "I fucking am moving on!" Howie blurted out. "Can't you read? My story is a work of art! The language, the plot, everything. My girlfriend is a fine arts painter and literature buff, I think she would have told me if it was crap." J relaxed and gave him an apologetic look. "Alright, so what do you want to do? What do you want from me?" J asked. "I want you to tell me you love the book and that you're going to send it to all your publicists and reviewers to make me critically acclaimed again." "I don't know, I don't know Howie, I still think you're missing something here." "What am I missing?"

J took a deep breath.

"It needs a more provocative plot, for one." Slow to react, Howie was now defenseless to J's onslaught. "Secondly, you need to get out, this writing is very interior, it's like you're cracking egg shells and walking on them. You haven't even been out for more than a year now... don't you realize what you're missing? You still wear the same old feather in your cap from years back, you're liable to become a parody of yourself Howard. You gott'a go out sometimes, go out and score something new." Howie was just about ready to self-destruct at the sound of J's words now, he started moving his lips, but no words could come out, like a steam-engine just blowing out hot air. "Oh, ya, oh ya, ya? Like this? The Boulevard?" He pulled out his wide screen phone that looked more like a tablet, and started furiously thumbing away at it. A video started to play.

It faded into a dark background, forming a perfect simulation of the Boulevard, like a videogame landscape. The game introduced footsteps tapping, the hustle and bustle of the street, the texture of all the boutiques, music playing from the clubs, the roar of engines, it was all coming to life on Howie's phone. "What is this?" J asked. No response. As the video progressed, it showed a girl to the right of the first-person view, in a digitized, whimsical voice, "I love it when I'm with you Howie, you know you make me feel like the happiest girl in the world when I'm with you...don't let go. Don't ever let go...' She said. Her voice faded, the screen became white. The video had a calming effect, it brought down the tension. "That was beautiful, Howie. How'd you do it, did you film it yourself?" "It's called augmented reality." He said. "Isn't it genius? I can go on the Boulevard, climb the Empire State Building, travel to Mars—"

"Yeah, but how did you get her voice, how did you get her voice so perfectly?" "I uploaded it from voicemails she left me. I got all kinds of scenarios on this thing. He flicked another clip as it faded in, again with the footsteps, this time a doorbell, and his ex-wife's voice, "Oh, come in..." A stranger's footsteps began to creak, mounting up steps. The video smash cut to the two of them hitting the sack in bed; grunts, moans, and before anything else, Howie's augmented-self barging in the bedroom. Seeing the philanderer about to defile his wife, he attacked him and started to beat him senselessly. "Stop, Howard, stop you're hurting him." With a sarcastic voice, "Stop? That's not what you were saying a minute ago! Poor, precious, lover boy!" One slug after another, the guy's face had become completely bloody. "Can't you stop him? He's killing the guy..." J asked with concern. "You mean me, can I stop me? Yeah... I can stop..." Howie squished the screen and pressed a command to stop the beating. "Here, you want me to stop the bleeding? Here." Howie began to control his augmented self in the video by sending him to run to the bathroom shower sink and grab a first-aid kit. "You're able to control it?" "Yea, isn't it great? I've got so many scenarios of me and her. "Can you download different people and voices?" "Yeah!" Howie replied, enthusiastically. "How would you be able to undress them though, can you get them naked?" J asked. "You really are a sick freak J. Anyways... I've got so many virtual life scenarios... all the ways I could have won my ex back; if only I could have stopped her from having an affair; if only I didn't blow my advance money on my second deal; if only I took her out more; if only we could have taken a vacation to the States, or somewhere else, anywhere, if only, if only... it gets me through the lonely weekends J."

"I had no idea..." He replied sympathetically. "You never heard of augmented reality?" "Well that too, but I had no idea you carried your break-up with you like that." "Yea, well I had no idea you were such a stiff when it came to publishing... you want me to write a musical? That's a laugh..." He let out a hearty cackle, "The last time I even wrote a play was in high school..." Before Howie could jump on his high horse, J replied, "And from what I heard, it went on to move audiences for more than a couple seasons." There was a sudden crystallized look between the two of them. "You've got to come back Howie. Play to your strengths, now's not the time to get caught up in a saucy love affair, it's time to move forward with your career, with your life. I'll work closely with you on this if you like, the next draft you send me, I'll be sure to take a close look at. I know that this will happen; it's just got to start here... and now. Here and now." "Alright, I hear what you're trying to say. And maybe I'll take your advice; I could go out on the Boulevard in real life." "I'll buy you your first round..." "Fair enough." "Sounds good Howie!" J exclaimed. Howie wore a serious grin on his face, finally, they had compromised. It was his greatest attempt at expressing happiness all day, he quickly stormed out of J's office.

As soon as Howie left the building J got on his phone to call Mellodia. He didn't want to let her slip through his hands; he didn't want to end up like Howie with a huge chip on his shoulder. The call went straight to voicemail, so he left her a message. Life would have to go on still, as depressing as his visit from Howie had been.

◊ ◊ ◊ ◊

On his drive home, J's mind kept racing about all the ways Mellodia was just letting him down easy. She was giving him a lot of mixed signals, and his phone wasn't ringing. The truth was she was busy, with life and going through the thick with Billy, and his touring band. Her moment of desperation passed and it was back to the daily grind.

The band got the song they wanted, Billy got what he wanted with Mellodia, and she got her dose of fame that she needed. She liked fame in small doses, it was like a controlled substance. For her Billy still wanted her to go on tour with him and the band, but after all his pleading and prodding, she still wasn't going to budge. Like hell was he going to be denied, plenty of groupies would bend over backwards just to get the same kind of offer, but she rejected for a couple of reasons. Mostly because of her work—having to take it with her could be a difficulty for that long on tour; as for her friend's band, her poor friend's band played the same shows week-in and week-out, the same old rock ballads and anthems. They were grateful to have her, and for getting them in Billy's studio, it wasn't any small order. With all the hit-making musicians he had recorded with, and the level of production, this single had the potential to catch on and spark interest for a new album.

Mellodia had a burst of energy, as soon as she got home from the studio office, she looked up her calendar her to-do list energetically. With a big black marker she swooshed off 'Record in award-winning studio'. She still had a few to-do's left, like, sky-diving, bungee jumping, produce a couple R&B songs, backpack Eastern Europe—she had already toured Western Europe—swim in a shark tank, go skinny dipping in the Atlantic—she had already gone skinny dipping once in the Pacific and the Mediterranean. She still had, 'Hook up with a celebrity', too. There was also, base jumping, ride a speedboat, dive for pearls, and take a road trip of the U.S., all on her to-do's. The diving was inspired by a life-long diver she had met while traveling. Still high on her list was going to the U.S. She was mainly fascinated with New York and L.A., good places to be in the music business, but also to experience country.

84

As she was dallying about, her phone suddenly rang. It was J's number. This time she picked up.

"Hello?" She whispered in a sexy voice. "Mellodia. It's J..." "I know..." "How are you?" "Fine..." "Okay, when am I going to see you?" "When?" "Yea, when? I want to see you. Maybe we can go to a movie?" "You mean on a date?" She replied. "Doesn't have to be a date..." Cutting through the silence, he continued.

— "What do you want to do?" He asked.

— "You're asking me, what I want to do?"

— "Ya..."

— "On a date...?" She asked.

— "Sure... what do you normally do, what do you do for fun?"

— "Lots of stuff... mainly music, travel, when I can, go on roller coasters." She laughed.

— "Oh ya? Roller coasters?" He asked.

— "So, what did you have in mind?" She prodded.

— "I don't know, we could grab a drink, have a nice dinner..."

— "Where?" She asked.

— "Well, there's a nice cove, we could go to the beach... we could go to a good restaurant nearby, it'd be nice."

— "Are you asking me out?"

— "You could say that... Why? Are you opposed to going out?"

— "No... I just want to know what you have in mind."

— "I'll make sure you're in bed by 11:00, I swear."

She laughed. She liked him, just didn't know him at all and felt he was going to come on too strong from how she met him and his persistent come-on's.

85

— "Well alright... when are you going to pick me up?"

— "Seven o'clock

— "Okay."

— "I'll give you a call later."

— "Okay, bye."

J picked up Mellodia at 7:10 in his fancy sports car. He had the inclination to drive fast, especially on the coast highway. They went to have dinner at a fusion restaurant, and had a few drinks together, after dinner they parked the car near the coastline, J pulled out one of his acoustic guitars from the trunk, and they strolled on the beach, eventually finding a cove nearby the water. It was lit up brightly by the moon, a romantic night. "Are you going to play that thing, or just wear it around your neck?" She asked. "Sure, I can play it." He replied. Smiling, he flipped around and strummed a few chords, picking away at the strings in a simple tune and smooth voice. His face was lit up like a young boy's. "Sounds nice." She said. "Thanks." He replied, "Oh, and I wrote you a song!" "You did?" She asked coyly. "That's so sweet of you." "Yeah! It goes like this..." He started playing the song he wrote when he was drunk and alone.

"Girl on the backstreets, you're the one I adore... If only I could see you more...

Searching, but what are we searching for? Running, but what are we running from?

Hey girl, you know... that you run in my heart. So, let's not get far apart...

Hey girl, you know that you were one in my heart. Right from the very start..."

She was a little moved, "I wrote that for you." Their starlit eyes stayed on each other. Without saying anything else she gave him a kiss on the lips. Sitting down high in the cove, they watched the stars and the white crests of the waves in the twilight of the moon. A man passed by, he was walking his dog. One of the dogs went up to J and Mellodia to sniff and lick their hands. "Hi there," Mellodia squealed. The dogs scampered off towards the sound of the crashing waves.

"So, do you visit here often?" She asked, hinting at his experience, and perhaps, how many girlfriends he had had. She assumed he had a lot of dates. "I come here on special occasions…" He replied. She checked him out for a moment, his starry eyes were laser-focused. His answer apparently satisfied her now palpitating heart, but she didn't know how to surrender to him, he had to make the first move. Another couple strolled by them, holding hands, but they didn't see them in the cove. They were whispering at each other, a lover's rhapsody. The guy picked her off her feet and carried her in his arms. "Oh, they're so cute." Mellodia remarked. "Yeah, I know…" J replied. She kept her gaze on his face, but he didn't look. "So, you write music?" She asked. "When I get a chance…" He replied. They looked right at each other, as if there was nothing to say. "I swear I saw you one night riding in that rocker's sports car. I could have sworn I saw you." Oh Billy's? Ya, I'm into the music business and what not. I'm not like a groupie or anything. He wants me to go on tour with the band. But I got work and my own band to manage."

"Oh ya?"

"Ya, they're No-One-And-Done', the punk rock band. "Oh ya, punk band? I've heard of 'em, been around a while…" "Yep. Going to try to make it mainstream. We just recorded a track in one of Billy's studios." "That's awesome." J replied.

Mellodia searched in his eyes and his face for a clue of who he was, what he was about. "How about you? What do you do?" She asked politely. "I work for a major book publisher. I set up all the book events and publicity for authors."

— "That sounds good…"

— "Ya. It keeps me busy, that's for sure… you do a lot of things for fun?"

— "I'm a bit of a thrill seeker, so yeah. I've been cliff diving, swam with sharks in Australia, I like to travel a lot, and party sometimes. You?"

— "Oh nice! Party too? I like to party too. I've traveled a little. I enjoy going to the pubs, a good drink or two, playing the guitar." "—And uh…"

An image of Melanie mixed with Howie raced through his mind, the augmented reality, the female worship…

— "…Those are some of the things I like."

— "That's nice…" She replied.

She squeezed his muscles tightly. Finally, J had her in his arms, this was happening, finally, it was happening… and then they kissed for the first time.

◊ ◊ ◊ ◊

Returning to J's apartment, they had one thing in mind, hit the soft linens, hard. Both were still buzzing from their date and pent up lust. Typically, J waited until he was already making love to start his intimate sweet talk, he whispered in her ear, "I need you so bad." He said. She was ogle-eyed as he worked on her, penetrating… she whimpered with each thrust and push.

She succumbed to her lust and physical romance. They started to push and pull, kneading each other's bodies, harder and harder. "Oh God… baby I want you…" He screamed. He brought her body to a steady rocking motion that made her weak. She had to quiet her emotions still letting out unbridled screams, "God, oh J, oh baby yes, yes, yes!"

Their lust was now springing, but Mellodia knew not to concede to any love, she wouldn't let that cat out of the bag so soon, or ever.

She let out a deep bellowing moan, nearly reaching a climax, as she started to weep and moan at the same time. It was like a beautiful sonnet they were writing together, their bodies swaying back and forth, she couldn't get a chance to breathe or rest, like a racehorse down to the wire; every slam, pull, and push was a measured ride to the finish. J kept her surprised with his sex to keep her in a heart-pounding, mind-bending fit of ecstasy.

In the heat of passion, J's intention was to come, but he wasn't wearing a condom. They were having sex with abandon, but Mellodia didn't seem to mind, she was aloof to it. Her punch-drunk mind was finally being relieved from the sex, on a cloud nine. The two of them were naked on J's bed, having beautiful sex, so much so, they may as well have died right there, wrapped in heavenly fine linens. Mellodia' s hair expanded out in full volume over the pillow and bed, she had one hand poised and extended like a gymnast sprawled out on the bed.

She looked up at the ceiling, wondering if she had to say anything or if J was eventually going to say something. Her eyes closed, frozen there, her chest rose up and down with each breath. Moments later, he started rubbing oils on her like a seasoned masseuse, spiritual music playing in the background. She loved it, and was only a little weirded out by it; she didn't say anything about it. It was other-worldly, bringing Mellodia to a lighter mood. Her feet tingled as J rubbed and kneaded, it all felt natural to her, but it made her look at herself and J a lot differently.

She became introspective by this tantric session, 'Did we not just have sex?' She thought. She started ruminating, an inner speech formed in her mind. She was disconnected, yet able to illuminate weird thoughts. 'I wonder what I would think if I didn't speak English?' She thought, 'Can we even not speak a language? How about Spanish, French… or Dutch? What does Dutch even sound like? I forget…'

J flipped her on her bare stomach and ass; her tits flopped on each side of her dainty ribcage. He began to carefully knead her back with the point of his elbow… "Oh, that feels good!" She said out loud. I don't even need thoughts, no one does.' She thought. "That feels sooo good, J, keep doing that." "Of course," He replied. He tried to focus on her back, he noticed her ass was tightening up, the kind of thing a wild sex fiend noticed in detail; it was like seeing an animal in its natural state, it commanded his attention. An unreal coloration, how perfectly shaped her ass was, how her skin formed goose bumps, they were becoming sensual and physically intimate.

She didn't know what she was thinking, her head was spinning, she could feel her thoughts, her senses were unwinding, her mind like that of a cat going in and out of sleep, the sort of dalliance that J craved in a woman. J accidently slid his elbow across her butt, and it jiggled a little. She turned over on high alert all of a sudden.

"So, what is the deal with you?" She said. 'This is it,' J thought. 'She's pissed. Show's over, I shouldn't have touched her butt. Oh shit, maybe she's onto me for not wearing a condom…' He thought. "I'm sorry, I didn't mean to, it was an accident…" He said. She no longer had goose bumps. "Hunh? No, I mean, what is the deal with you saying I'm your goddess?" "When?" "Who even says that? Are you some kind of fringe hippie or—?" "I just thought that at the time. I… I don't know what else to say…" "So, you think I'm a goddess now?" She asked furiously. "I don't know. No?" "That's because you don't even know me. What kind of person does this? What kind of ritual is this anyway?" J was a little bit disheartened; the vibe of pure sex was turning into a game of charades. "I'm sorry, I don't know… how can I make it up to you?" "Make it up to me? You're like a snail under my heel, are you some kind of masochist or something?" "Don't freak out, it's nothing it's just part of a healthy lifestyle regiment. Nothing is going to happen, just relax…" "I don't know, it

89

just kind of worries me, I've never seen a guy do this before. It's really freaking me out."

He replied in earnest, "Don't worry. Just let me take care, it helps relieve the stress, and should feel good… doesn't it?" "Well, ya, you were kind of amazing…" "See?" "But you swear you're not going to do something crazy?" She asked. He giggled innocently. "Of course, not… unless you want me to handcuff you and tie you up." She looked at him dead serious for an instant. "I'm kidding…" "Not funny." She replied.

The irony was she did have sex involving handcuffs and whips before; she just wasn't used to the crazy monk rituals and she got a little scared diving this deep into his love-making. They both looked at each other. The two of them were such gabby guts at times, yet so insular and collected with their intimacy. They hardly knew each other as far as background and life experiences were concerned. That's not to take away the fact that they had made a deep, intimate connection. Until J had accidently slid his elbow across her butt, they hadn't exchanged more than a few words. Nor did they need to, the connection was there, and it was deep, somehow.

Mellodia left J's apartment walking on air, maybe she had a new relationship, maybe she didn't, but the sex was great and she had the boy under her heel. Although he was zany in his rituals, the post-sex massage was also great. 'He'll call me,' she thought, 'for sure, he'll call me.'

◊ ◊ ◊ ◊

Valentine's Day was quickly approaching and the only thing going on in J's mind was 'Melli, Melli, Mellodia; mommy, mommy, mommy.' He was gaga for her, for the special day he was going to surprise her at work by bringing her flowers. She had been immersed with finishing an album with an alternative band, so she barely saw J during these times. But they still had planned to do something that weekend.

Finishing up for a record release, the studio had top-of-the-line equipment, enough breathing room for the lot of them, but the reason they were going across town was a leading recording engineer. The mood was professional, a lot different from the whiskey-guzzling dark rooms Mellodia was used to.

On his way there, J had to navigate with the help of a GPS system, and even then, it was all very shifty with back country roads and dead zones. What was great about road trips was he had a luxury sports car that handled fuel well. Gathering dust and dirt along the open country road, J had a full deck of CD's of rock-n-roll, punk rock, electronic and country to get him through the boring drive. With the smell of new leather in his car, a big stuffed teddy bear and a bouquet of roses, J was feeling like a million bucks and he was ready to wow Mellodia to take her out for an early weekend. He had the reservations planned with a bread & breakfast in the country.

Finally, he had found the studio off the beaten path. When he got to the studio, he wasn't sure where he was, or if he had made a wrong turn, for instance. The outside was black, and the building had little contrast to one another. He rang the doorbell after a tense minute he was greeted by one of the band. "Is Melli here?" "Yeah, hold on, let me get her." J just followed him through a narrow corridor leading into the main recording room where they were finishing up. He glowed in the room with his hands full of red roses and a big stuffed teddy bear. Melli was so surprised, she was in shock. All the renewed anticipation of the weekend beating out of her little chest. "J…? I can't believe you're here! All this way?!" "Just wait until you see the room I booked for us, we're going to have dinner at a chateau tomorrow, fresh oysters and champagne. I got everything booked and ready to go."

A loud, distant thumping, and the wailing of alternative music sounded in the background. Like most alternative rock, it had a lot of angst, but the band was recording an upbeat album for the most part. Yet, they still needed to liven the mood a little. "Just a minute J." Melli set her gifts down and grabbed her notes while the song continued playing. She jotted down a couple notes and started talking to the sound engineer. "Can we make the hook a little more uppity? The label says they want it to stand out." "Uppity? Like how do you mean?" She started moving her hands in conversation; from the point of view of the guitarist he could see they were having a full-blown conversation. After the third chorus, he ripped off his headphones and simply stopped playing. Melli screamed at him, "Hey what are you doing?!" "I'm distracted. I can't even think." he said. "What do you mean? You were doing great…" "I can't play like this. I need a break." He set his guitar down and ran out of the studio, brushing Melli off of him.

Hanging out on a spare sofa, J just looked at Melli, "Hey." She went to embrace him. "It'll be just a little while, hope that's okay." "That's fine." He replied. "You think I can get some time?" He started strumming on the guitar. "Ya…" "Sure, knock yourself out." He began gearing up like a kid in a candy shop, acoustic guitar in hand. Everyone went outside to check on their frustrated band mate.

J was fiddling away with the guitar, playing a few chords, completely consumed by it. Melli was outside checking up on the band.

J noticed a sound guy was still on deck, he motioned to him and asked him, "Turn me up?" The sound guy coolly turned up a few levels on the sound board and gave him a thumb's up. J started playing the song he wrote when he was thinking of Mellodia.

"Hey girl, you know you run in my heart… so let's not get far apart. Searching, but what are we searching for? Running, but what are we running from? Hey girl you know that you're one in my heart, right from the very start… It's you that I want; and I'm losing my front, for good…"

He kept playing his heart out, finishing up the song; no response. Anticlimactically, he walked out of the sound room to see what was going on with the band. They were all having a cigarette; basically pow-wowing like there was no tomorrow. He was merely a shadow among their constant chatter. He cut their conversation and bumped Melli.

— "I'm gonna head out and make sure we got everything ready for tomorrow.

— "Okay, yeah sorry…"

— "No problem, can you meet me there?"

— "Sure."

— "Alright great. Let me give you a kiss." She squeezed and kissed him for a long time.

— "I'll call you a little later."

— "Sounds great." She replied.

He shook hands with the band. "Hope I didn't distract you too much." J said to the guitarist.

"No, you're fine." He replied, looking somewhat catatonic. J stormed out and shamelessly started up his sports car in front of them. Speeding away, they were left with the sound of J's engine, still puffing on cigarettes.

92

They seemed tense and stressed out, yet beneath all the stress, Mellodia was still excited for her weekend. This is what she needed to rev up the band, and wrap things up for the project.

"C'mon baby, let's get back in there and finish this thing up." She was looking more than ready to pep the band back up. Taking a couple deep breaths, she was fired up like a fresh cup of coffee in contrast to a catatonic marching band before her. She had the energy and the right stuff to finish this album the way their major label wanted it to be done. It was just going to take a lot of work.

◊ ◊ ◊ ◊

The next day, Mellodia asked for J's room at the bed and breakfast, she had the teddy bear he gave her clutched in her palms. The concierge greeted her, "Room 1020, eleventh floor," he said. She rode her way up the elevator with a fine gentleman, he was carrying a dozen bouquet of roses. They both looked at each other curiously. "You meeting your valentine?" The stranger asked. "Yes." She replied, "As a matter of fact I am... and you?" "My wife..." "Oh, I see. Where's your ring?" He gave her a pregnant look of obvious infidelity. They were nearly at their floor now when he sneaked a kiss on her, and managed to whisper a sweet nothing in her ear. He then slipped on his wedding ring discretely, it was all very suave. She was noticeably stirred up, shocked and breathless from the surprise display of affection.

Off the elevator she went, like a breath of fresh air. She jammed over to J's room, and rapped at the door. She could hear smooth R&B in the background. "Who is it?" J asked. "It's Me, Melli." She said giggling infectiously. J opened the door, welcoming her with a big hug. The mood was set, candles lit, dinner prepared. a pair of smiles were beaming across both their faces. "Get in here you!" He hollered. "You want a glass of wine?" He asked gently. "That'd be great." "Or champagne, if you want, we have champagne too..." "Whichever..." "Save the bubbly?" He remarked. "Bubbly." She said, she couldn't help but giggle. She motor-boated her lips with her fingers. "You okay?" He started giggling with her. "A long day... but yeah, I'm okay, I just couldn't wait." They sat down and chimed their wine glasses with cheers.

The bath had bubbles drawn in the tub, with scented candles and bathroom all lit up, overlooking the countryside. Mellodia lay with her back against J's chest as he massaged her shoulders and neck. "You're so tense. You feeling a little better now, at least?" "Ya... oh yeah, right there, don't stop, that feels amazing." She replied. "So, we're doing oysters and champagne this weekend, at the bar, but you also do have a surprise from me." "I do?! Oh my god, what is it?" "I'll tell you later, it's a surprise,

93

wait until tomorrow." She turned around to straddle his body, and gave him a lip-sucking kiss. "Tell me now!" "It's a surprise." He said. "Full of surprises, I used to like surprises…" She gasped.

She started working on his pectorals, getting her body rubbing against his. "I can't believe you drove all the way just to see me, that made me so happy J. A pregnant look…"I would have driven a hundred miles to see you Melli, are you kidding?" Trying to catch her breath she put her hands on her chest. "Really?" She replied. She looked at him carefully. He didn't want to seem so desperate, but it was true, no distance was too far to see her, whether she knew it or not, she was a great catch to J, and he cared for her deeply.

The next day they went into town they had some chocolate at a chocolate bar, and walked around the park, watching all the other couples and families. It was free-spirited with rolling green hills near the countryside.

At dinner, they had fresh seafood, oysters and champagne, just as J promised. It was enough food to feed more than the two of them, really. J kept drinking and drinking, and so did she. They had their rounds of laughs, buzzing from all the alcohol; it was all very exciting, but beneath the surface J was bored. He felt like they were going to become a lonely couple, he could sense she was feeling the same thing. Yet they didn't say anything, just enjoyed the moment while it lasted.

Their heads knocked one another as they fell into the ever-so-cushioned mattress. He was sure to wear a condom this time, but he probably could have got away with slipping it off again, she was still quite a bit buzzed. It was the usual, "Pull my hair… give it to me harder," kind of sex. And then they passed out.

In the middle of the night, Melli suddenly fell ill, waking up in a terrible, cold sweat from bed, she ran to the bathroom sink, vomiting badly.

Quickly, he ran into the kitchen and filled a mug with water from the tap, putting it in the microwave to quickly boil for hot tea. He shuffled through the cupboards; the earl grey fell out of the tea box, so he grabbed a couple of green teabags and popped the mug out of the microwave, mixing it with honey. Running back to the bathroom Melli was now occupying the bathroom. "You alright?" He asked. "Sick right now." It was 4 a.m. in the morning and they had a big day ahead of them. "You want me to get you anything?" "No, I'll be alright." She replied.

They didn't sleep all night. Daylight slowly broke through the wee hours, J hadn't slept for more than a few minutes and Mellodia was trying to drain out her sickness, constantly taking hot showers.

It was a miserable night, but Mellodia had recovered a little from taking hot showers. J was getting that same sinking feeling that they were going to become a dreary couple. The next morning, they joined other hotel patrons for a continental breakfast. Most of the people there were families and married couples sharing their contempt for love, internally and outwardly. "You see this?" A spouse asked Mellodia, pointing to his ring, "You're looking at a dead-end relationship." They just looked at each other for a second, 'Is this guy for real?' J thought. "Why, are you looking at my girlfriend? You can talk to me if you have something to say." J said defensively, giving off just enough heat to cause a scene. The guy looked at J like he wanted to kill him with a hacksaw. The strange man stood up as soon as his wife came back and kept staring at J. "He's funny." Melli said lightheartedly. "Yeah, if by funny, you mean idiotic." J replied. "You're funny too." J didn't have an answer, just a hearty look. She looked right back at him, as if to say, 'What the hell got into you?'

Looking at Mellodia, J had a change of heart as he always did when he was near her. "You ready to go?" He asked. But instead of a sweet smile, she just rolled her eyes. "Yeah sure…" Letting him know her heart wasn't there.

J carried a big camera that strapped onto his neck, he looked like a tourist as they hopped into an open touring Jeep. They were going through what was basically a late billionaire's backyard turned to a wild nature habitat. Eighty-thousand acres of open land, ranging from desert habitat to lush forest, it was remarkable how the environment could change so profoundly. From snakes and lizards, the Jeep sped through to meet a herd of buffalo and a few giraffes. The giraffes seemed to smile as they ate green leaves off the trees in the distance.

The tour guide drove through the terrain, pointing to some of the animals, "You see over there? Look! You se'er over there? That giraffe's giving birth!" He said excited, J unsheathed the lens of his camera and started to point and shoot. "We'll get a little closer to see this miracle in action, but please no cameras, the mother giraffe is in labor. They cautiously neared the giraffe, who was awkwardly giving birth… the baby giraffe was finding its way out. "Here she goes! Now be very quiet, she can hear us…"

There was a loud 'thump'. The baby giraffe fell to the ground from her mother's womb, five feet in the air. It was a spectacle, to say the least. Melli looked at J in amazement, her eyes wide as globes, his pupils narrowed like reticules in focus.

Slowly, they passed through the jungle, parting their blessings from a safe enough distance, they passed zebras at 35 miles per hour, but in the wild, it felt more like 135 miles per hour. They made their journey through this entire space, the bamboo forest, the redwood forest, and finally the majestic French gardens where they were to get special spa treatment. A motorcade of three red Jeeps rolled through the marbled entrance. "Hope you enjoyed the tour of the arboretum and wildlife habitat. Have a great weekend!" The tour guide tipped his hat and signed off with a graceful bow. Knapsack in hand, J and Mellodia breathed the spring air, making their way through the pearly front entrance.

The couples spent the rest of their retreat away from each other, the guys with guys, and gals with gals. There was a lot of open space, luxurious Italian marble, remarkable detail on every column and hallway. There was an arid ambiance that hinted at quiet opulence. The estate was fit for royalty.

The ladies were in white robes, lavishing away in the spa, the warm glow and reflection from the Italian marble shined gently against their skin. They were in high spirits chatting up a storm in this pristine setting.

One of the women, a queen bee of a woman, kept chatting, "My man keeps me well pampered, but I still have boyfriends on the side...he doesn't even know." She said. "Damn, that's cold." The queen bee started to flaunt pretentiously. "...Well when the sex gets boring. How could you not? You don't have lovers..?" "Well, since you ask... it's a fling but my husband and I have been married for years, and he has his girlfriends as well... but no, I don't have boyfriends." She said, emphasizing the plural form. The four of them laughed, except for Melli, she was in her own world, daydreaming, her feet barely in the hot Jacuzzi.

'What would it be like to have multiple boyfriends?' Melli thought. A question mark was written all over her precious face. "What's your name?" The woman asked. "Melli..." "Why are you over there by yourself girl? You look a bit shy. What's wrong?" A blank look was written on Melli's face. "Poor thing." Another boisterous wife stared at her until she finally looked back. Her face was full of exfoliating cream. "You don't want to jump into the hot Jacuzzi with us? You're still in your robe, barely poking your toe, girl. Let's see you get in here." "I don't like hot water." Melli replied. Actually, she just didn't want to get involved in their mess.

96

They seemed like too merry of wives, ones always fixing to raise hell on their husbands. "Are you two newlyweds?" "No." Mellodia replied. "Wow, really? He must really have plans for you. Most of our hubbies are still just making it out of the doghouse." They erupted in laughter. "I had locked my husband out one time. He had to sleep in the shed." "I've seen your husband. I would never lock his ass out. That man is fine." She nodded her head to make her point. "Yeah, well you get tired of 'em." "Uh-hunh," they nodded. "It's always the same routine. They come home, want their dinner, want sex, then they roll over and fall asleep—hopefully don't snore—and when they are up, they're in their own little world. Don't ever get married Mellodia. Just stay young and single girl. That way you can at least enjoy your life."

She just laughed it off, it was barely her first outing with J and already she was in the lion's den with a bunch of conniving housewives. 'What am I going to do?' She thought. 'If I marry, I'll be secure, I can pursue my career.' So she thought. "If you really want to know my advice—marry a doctor, they have the most secure incomes and they always take care of you." Melli just darted her eyes from the wife's face to the ceiling and back to her face. She couldn't believe they were having this conversation; she was out of her element, it was more of a retreat to a salon than a true vacation like this.

Back in the hotel room, Melli's room was littered with lavish room service with a full spread of food. Both her and J lied around like lions in a heap. They flipped through the channels and bounced ideas off each other. A runner came up to the door in earnest. "Room service." He hollered. When Melli opened the door, she was presented a covered platter. "Surprise!"

"What is this?" Mellodia asked in wonder. She opened the lid to reveal what was inside, it was two plane tickets. "I made reservations for us. So you can visit the states." "Oh my god!" She cried out. She was speechless. She embraced him tightly. "Will you go with me this summer?" "Of course, I'd love to, you know how badly I want to take a vacation!" "We'll fly into New York first, start our vacation from there. It'll be great." He said enthusiastically. She had stars in her eyes.

◊ ◊ ◊ ◊

Summer had rolled around quickly, and with record heat; now J and Mellodia had time to escape on their dream vacation. A vacation for two months meant no steady work for that time, which was daunting, but J felt it was going to pay off. His intention was to eventually marry Mellodia, if there ever was a chance.

They would be in New York in eight hours and begin their vacation together. The entire thing was planned for the next two months. First it was New York, then L.A.—a road across the map—then back to New York. To make the most of their vacation, they had booked a couple industry events, since the bread and butter of building their business was networking, this was a must.

They purposely sat apart from each other on the flight, like an old veteran couple. The young gentleman sitting next to Mellodia kept looking at her curiously. His significant other noticed he was distracted, so she kept prodding him, bugging him with little things to keep his attention. There was such curiosity and wonder Mellodia inspired in him. The whole time J would watch the young man's gazing at Mellodia for what seemed like a full hour. Finally, the young man dared to ask, after catching her attention, "Sorry, but I can't help to ask... you look so familiar... what is your name?"

"Mellodia..." She replied. "Ah, now there's a familiar name." "Familiar?" Without skipping a beat, he continued. "I'm Beau, this is my girlfriend Sara." "Hi..." Mellodia said. "How about you, you have a boyfriend?" His girlfriend nudged him. "Stop it, Jesus!" He poked and tickled her, she started moving squirming around in her seat and squealed as he tickled her. "Stop... stop..." He mocked. "You're going to get it!" She said, putting up her fists. He turned back towards Mellodia and continued, "So... do you or don't you have a boyfriend?" The whole time J was watching this stranger's fascination with Melli play out. "Yes..." She replied. "Ah! And so, where the hell is he? I don't see how a boy could ever leave you alone, you're so pretty. I would never leave you alone." "He's sitting over there." Melli said, pointing across the aisle. J was sitting in awe, just watching this spectacle from a safe distance, almost as a voyeur.

"Oh, I see, keeping your distance? We would do the same thing, but this one..." he poked his girlfriend, "She doesn't trust me." "Stop it." She said, "You're lying!" He said. "No, honestly we're an open-ended relationship." She gave him a cross look, "Will you shut up already?" "Fine, go ahead babe, look this woman in the eye, look—Mellodia, right? Look Mellodia in the eye and tell her we're not swingin' from the vines." Beau was now as warm-blooded as a furry mammal. His girlfriend was all cracked up in the face, the freak inside her tried to escape, but she couldn't help but to laugh hysterically in front of Mellodia when her boyfriend challenged her to admit the truth.

They were only five hours from JFK airport. Mellodia and J just soaked up this crazy couple's convo. J, the voyeur that he was, looked on from a safe distance. He was so mesmerized by his girlfriend. The mannerisms of her face, the way she shut off the world around her, making it seem like he was the only one who could see her, how the world revolved around her, it amazed him. Mellodia could read the woman like an open book; they were both freaks of the same kind, Mellodia just a bit more reticent. "So, where are you visiting in the city?" Beau asked. "Oh well, we're going all over, New York, then going to L.A. for a little while, going to some music industry events." "Oh ya? Like the Grammy's? My cousin's a producer, we went last year, in fact—we went to the Grammy's, didn't we Sara?" His girlfriend gave him a sour look. "Yeah, it's alright," He continued, "the after-party was the most fun, the after-party… Right boo?" He asked jokingly. His girlfriend just rolled her eyes. "Seriously though, we should meet up, you guys and us." Mellodia glanced at him a little scared. Then she turned her focus away, shut off from Beau's pressing conversation. "What's your number?" He asked, he pulled out his phone and furiously typed in it as she told it to him. "Great! We'll give you guys a call after we land!" He smiled, and comically put on some head phones, like nothing happened at all, tuning out the world, still sitting right next to her. Mellodia turned her head to look at J, giving a curious look as if to ask, 'Who are these crazy people?!'

◊ ◊ ◊ ◊

As people started de-planning, Mellodia woke up startled, as if out of a nightmare. J nudged her, "C'mon, we're here." He said. "Let's go!" "We're here?" She asked. "Where, here?" "We just landed." J said. She still tried to gain consciousness from a powerfully deep sleep. She had dreamt J left her for a stewardess in L.A. It was vivid and hard to shake, like being under a spell.

Once awake, they practically leapt off the plane. Gripping Mellodia' s hand, J walked as fast as he could in excitement. They flew through customs and hailed a taxi, Mellodia closed her eyes for what seemed like only a second. She woke up at their hotel room. They arrived at their hotel in a New York minute.

The city was surreal. Faint sounds of the loud, obnoxious street permeated their 30th floor suite. It was like watching a circus from a rising blimp, everything just seemed to fade out from this distance.

"Hey Melli…?" J asked. She had her face pressed to the glass window. "Yes, what?" She replied. "You know how we always wanted to make our own video, like a sex tape?" "What? What do you mean always? We've only talked about it once or

99

twice…" She replied cautiously. "No, I know, but we never really have yet." "Why are you bringing this up? I'm cold. I'm hungry… and why are you staring at me like that?" "I'm not staring." He answered defensively. "I looked up this photographer who does great work in the city. He can make a great video for us. She approached him nearer, feigning affection, she grazed his face. "Honey that's so great…"

"I knew you would like it, he does specialized photographs, you know with the lens…" "Sounds great, J…" "What's wrong?" He asked. "I'm hungry. Where are we eating?" "I don't know, you see anything good on the room service menu?" She just gave him a cold, blank stare. "What?" He quipped. "I'm fucking hungry J! Can't you understand?" He looked at her blankly. So, I asked, what do you want for room service…?" She guffawed, disgusted by him. "You don't ever understand me, it's always about you." She belted out. "What?! Of course, I understand you." "You don't!" She screamed, pacing back to the window. The jetlag, being overwhelmed by the city, all the reminders of how they were in a relationship that was not really meant to be; it crept underneath her skin. "All you want is sex, and to feed your obsessions!" She yelled. She started to cry, pawing at the window, looking out at the New York skyline. "Okay, we'll go out to eat…" He said, completely clueless. He raised the phone and began to dial, Mellodia just sank to the floor, starting to pout.

◊ ◊ ◊ ◊

"Go ahead and get comfortable," The photographer said, focusing his lens, he carried a tripod larger than his body. It was an intimate setting that portrayed J and Mellodia on a waterbed with floral notes and linens. "Let me know when you're ready." He added. "We're ready." J said, "Right?" He asked. "Sure." Mellodia answered.

They went straight to it, first undressing each other, a few sensual kisses… Mellodia made eye contact with the camera as she rode J. A cool breeze came through the window, the sounds of the city emanating in the bedroom suite. It made them even more naked. The photographer was so excited, the camera kept shuttering. He rallied them on like a red-carpet event. Their carnal senses were lit, the whole time they were focused on each other's eyes in a missionary position. With the occasional moan, there was no acting, they were both feeling quite a different arousal with this quiet beast rallying them on, his camera in hand. The only difference of having the photographer was the added risqué, a sense of exhibitionism; but, of course, J never came. Mellodia owned him, she was a starlet for the camera, and even egged him on for more. J just collapsed on her body and had to roll off her after a good amount of sex. She looked

100

into the camera with her arms crutched underneath her boobs. "That's enough." J blurted out. He couldn't take it, she was a pornstar suddenly, it was pushing his buttons too hard. He just wanted to sleep and move on. "Can you leave us be?" J asked the photographer. The photographer swiftly exited the room, J was no longer the dominant force, he felt demeaned and outshined by Mellodia. "Are you happy now?" She asked him. "I'm tired, that's all."

"I kinda liked it." She said. "I could tell." He said, stuffing his head in. "Where are we eating? She asked. "I'm hungry." "I don't know." "Let's go somewhere nice." She said. "Whatever you want, whatever you want Melli…"

The two of them went out to the city to eat at a nice restaurant. Seated at the bar, they ordered fresh sushi. Mellodia was getting a lot of attention, as much as would be expected after conquering a sex tape. J was getting nothing; he was like a slug, a turtle in a shell. Of course, this made him feel worse about the whole ordeal. And, of course, it made Mellodia look more. They didn't know, J could write a lyric with the feather in his cap. And he had more than one. They didn't know he was J Willemson, well-known around town, and could talk the skin off a sausage. Had they known, they would imitate him, they would get the girl's number and walk on, call the girl and take her to the flat, and seal the deal. That's if they were even willing and able. Because there was one goal in life and that was to get the girl. The only problem now was he already had her.

The malaise from watching his girl in action, knowing he was just a tortoise in a rabbit chase. It was a pain he didn't feel when he was on top of the game. Now it was the pain of becoming someone else, something else. It was game over, but not for her, she was now this paragon of a sexual woman. 'How does it come to this?' He thought. What a cruel way to live, all the innocence just washed away in painful voyeurism.

She didn't even try to put on a front. Every guy was now looking at her in her ravishing eyes; she gave them the time of day, the right of way. J was just a fucking lampshade now. He was just a freaking freak. Another barrage of filthy looks from a pack animal at the bar, 'She wouldn't, would she? What are you looking at?' J thought. It was the Melli show, and it was all free. The woman he would beg to marry was going to make him suffer a lot differently than he thought. J was suddenly at a loss.

◊ ◊ ◊ ◊

101

The next morning J crawled out of bed, Mellodia was already up and doing her make-up. The phone rang. "Hello?" J answered. It was the photographer. "Yeah, yeah, we're here— Okay great, that would be wonderful— Un-hunh—Okay, thanks." "Who was that?" Mellodia asked, applying her lipstick in the mirror. "That was the photographer, he said the photos are done." "Oh, great!" "He's willing to do another portrait shoot of us, free-of-charge." "Oh ya? How exciting!" "He's stopping by in a few."

J dragged himself into the shower, wiping the sleep out of his eyes as he turned on the hot water. The phone rang again, it was Mellodia' s cell phone ringing this time. "Hello this is Mel..." She said in a loud voice. She thought it was her work or someone in the band calling her. "Oh hi...! Yes, we made it here okay. How about you? —The neighbors from the airplane..." She whispered to J. "Good..." She replied, "Okay! Why don't you come visit us here at the 'W' for lunch... room 1020, 30th floor... or just call... okay bye!" Mellodia hung up the phone, she was buzzing again.

J stepped out of the shower as Mellodia was still getting fixed up. "You remember those two from the airplane?" Mellodia asked. "Yeah, what about them? They called?" "Yes, they want to see us at around 1:00, isn't that exciting?!" "Yeah! Actually, that is." He replied, "Do they know how to get here?" "I guess so, I told them where we're staying, they have my number anyways..."

Before long the photographer made his way back to the hotel, they huddled around his huge camera to look at the digital prints. "It looks good!" Mellodia shouted. He gave them a DVD and some blown up photos of their intimate experience. "If you don't mind, I'd like to do a couple more portraits of you." Mellodia looked at J, "How nice!" She answered. The photographer started setting up.

There was a loud knock at the door, "Oh it must be them." Mellodia said. "I'll get it. She jammed to the front door and opened it. "Hi!" The couple raised their hands; Beau had a bottle of wine in his hands. "So how are you lovin' New York?" He asked. "Oh my god, so fab!" Melli replied. "I'm so glad you guys came to see us. We were getting lonely by ourselves..." As they stepped into the door they noticed the photo shoot, "Are we interrupting something?" Sara asked. "Oh no, this is just... well we were just, we were just doing a portrait." J waved to them making his way into the room. "Glad, you could visit." He cheered. "Of course, our pleasure! So, your first time in the city!" Beau said. "What have you got planned for today?"

J tried to explain what it all was, "Oh, well, right now we're doing a portrait…" The photographer moved in to make his introduction, "I'm Tomas, I do live intimate photo shoots." They smiled. He left them a business card and went to make his exit. "Thanks for the shoot, and feel free to call me when you have time." "Okay, thank you." J said. Tomas grabbed his gear and left. "Intimate photo shoots, eh?" Beau asked. "What is that?" J looked a little shy, he didn't respond. "We did a personal sex tape, basically." Mellodia said. "A sex tape?! Wow, there you go!"

She started him up, because Beau couldn't stop shooting off about sex tapes and sex in general. J couldn't stop thinking the worst thoughts, most of which he concealed. Staring at Sara, he couldn't help but to think of her and Beau and Melli, lounging away in bath robes. She caught him checking her out, and winked, as if to say, 'If you like what you see…' J was far too gone by now, he was on his own planet, tuning Beau out, who kept harping on about people and their sex tapes and all the other in's and outs of good photography. "I was good friends with a photographer. That photographer, Tomas…? He's good. I can tell."

J fantasized about Melli and Sara kissing. He was already having a dress rehearsal in his daydream. "So, what do you say J?" Beau insisted. "Say what?" He woke up a little. "You think we can look at your portraits?" J hesitated a bit, "Sure…" He replied. "Don't be so forward Beau, they just made this…" Sara said. "No, it's fine." J assured her. Deep down he was a little nervous, this was their first sex tape, and he and Melli were still innocent to all this. J threw on the DVD, hiding his feelings. Their nude bodies flashed up on the TV, first their black-and-whites, then their blurred-out images. It was a beautiful medley of intimacy, not as bad or embarrassing as J had initially feared.

Beau was sitting uncomfortably close to Mellodia, he had scooted in next to her. It made him slightly infuriated; it was just too close for comfort. Turning to Mellodia, Beau looked her straight in the eyes and said, "I love it. I love your portraits." "Thanks." "We gotta get out of here soon." J interjected. "Gotta get? Where?" Mellodia asked. "Well, we're not just going to spend the entire day in this hotel room, are we?" He said furiously. "Where are you going?" Sara asked. "To the restaurant, the club, I don't know, somewhere. "Oh nice," Sara replied, "Well, we have tickets to the opera, if you care to join us later." "That's be really nice." Mellodia insisted. Melli got up and clasped Sara's hands. "We'll just have to get ready, and meet up with you—." "Oh, you can get ready here; I have all kinds of make-up. Check it out. The room's so bright and big." They left the room like a couple of school girls. Beau shook his head to J, as if to say 'women…'

"So how has your stay been so far?" Beau asked. "It's been alright." J answered, still fidgeting his hands in his pockets nervously. "What's wrong?" "Nothing wrong." J assured him. He kept playing nervously with his pocket, however. "What do you have in your pocket?" A scared glassy look peered back at Beau. "You seem nervous." J reluctantly pulled out a jewel case, Beau's eyes widened at the sight of a huge ring. "Holy shit, you're proposing?" "Shh! I was going to tonight at dinner, I think I'm going to wait, though, I'm pretty sure she'll say 'yes', but she's still really scared."

While the gals were putting on their make-up, J seemed to be having a quiet, normal conversation. "You guys monogamous?" "Yeah." J replied bluntly. "Well, that's funny," Beau said. "Why's that funny?" "This is your first sex tape?" "We've been meaning to make one for a while." "Let's take a look at it."

J hesitated. Beau gave him a look. Unafraid, almost predatorily, Beau could get away with it with his casual charm. "Hold on." J went to grab the DVD. He couldn't find it; really, he was pretending not to find it. He was a little nervous. "I'll be right back." He chuckled. Making his escape, he was reminded of his private school days, the cruel little peccadilloes he and his friends would drum up, Beau reminded him of one of his old schoolmates.

J stormed into the make-up room. "Hey Melli." The two of them turned their heads in awe, "Can't you knock?" "Knock?" He replied, "There's no door..." "What do you want?" She asked. "Where's the DVD?" "DVD? I don't know, are you two at all ready?" J nodded, "Beau wants to see the tape..." "Okay, well wait some other time; I don't know how to set up the DVD player anyway. Need to call room service or someone." Strolling back into the living area, J rejoined Beau. "No dice. Probably later..." "Alright, no problem." Beau replied. "Are the gals ready? Or are they putting on a cake?" J smiled. "Yeah, that'll be the day!" Beau laughed out heartily. "No, they're about ready. C'mon, let's go!"

◊ ◊ ◊ ◊

At dinner, J didn't do a lot of talking, he was still nervous. And although they didn't eat much, they had a bottle of wine that Beau brought. Beau and Sara were chatting a lot, about their experiences in the city, their likes and dislikes, they had quite a bit of experience.

After dinner, the four of them went to the opera at the Met. There was something about an Italian opera that spoke to them on such a last-minute notice. The taxi ride and the city whirled past them as they chatted in their taxi.

The magnificence of the whole scene crept up into them at the met. "What is the name of the Opera?" J asked. "La Traviata" Beau replied, somewhat austerely. They looked at each other, suddenly out of place. "Looks like people are trotting in to see Traviata." Mellodia looked at her ticket as J rushed in the front door, the rest followed, but Mellodia was stuck staring at her ticket. She seemed lost. Inside the Met, J searched for their seats, but he still led the way. He glanced at his tickets. "We're going up." He said. Beau and Sara passed him, glancing in wonder. "Where's Melli?" J asked. "I thought she was behind us…" Beau replied. "Ah well, she'll find us, she's got a seat next to me anyhow." Up they went, all the way to the nosebleeds. Passing all the gloriously fashioned New Yorkers was like passing a million-dollar yacht in a small tug boat. They dragged themselves up nearly all the way to the ceiling, up every floor, in circles, all starry-eyed and confused. Finally, they found their seats—but still no Melli.

A curtain call signaled the show was about to start, and they had already seated themselves, J furiously called Melli, but she was thoroughly lost. As the opera started, J saw her in the corner of his eye, walking up the rows. She yelped, "I was on the opposite side of the theater." "Shhhh!" He hushed her up with an irritated finger pointed to his lips. J didn't even look at her. They had all dragged their bodies up this theater, and already it felt like they had bloody noses.

◊ ◊ ◊ ◊

During intermission, the four of them rushed down the hall for drinks, they ordered a simple stout while the crowds were drinking different shades of red wine and bubbly. "What do you think about the Verdi?" Beau asked, J nodded him off, not able to hide his misery. "I can't understand a word their saying." Beau continued. "You just follow the story, hun." Sara said. You know, this one's about…well I don't entirely remember…"

"Yeah, I guess…" J replied. "How do they wear all those costumes without getting so hot?" Beau asked. "It's probably a lot cooler down on the stage then it is where we're sitting," Sara remarked. After people made their way back, the four of them followed like a bunch of phantoms stumbling back to their seats. The lights went down, and the curtain call led to the second act. Cutting through the sound of the orchestra, and the booming voices of the tenors, was someone snoring his brains out, next to them. It was as if only their section of the theater could hear this obnoxious man snoring.

Yet, everyone—including Mellodia—couldn't help but to bust up laughing at this obvious distraction, everyone except J, his face tightened in disgust. His pretentious nature was coming out during the opera. 'Why is everyone laughing', he thought to himself, 'this guy is totally ridiculous'. It was only a distraction to their section of the theater. Apparently, the man who was snoring was alone, because no one ever woke him up; he had fallen asleep throughout the rest of the show until catching himself in his own drool and sneeze.

The final act was far too oozing in drama to worry about any distractions. After the fat lady sang, nearly blowing the top off the theater, the final scene left the audience in wild applause, some giving a standing ovation, and even the sleeping man woke up to give a cheer.

There was an awkward, tired silence in the cab on the cab ride home. Beau had to break the ice. "What a great show, that's probably the best one we've seen in a long time." "Yeah." Sara replied. "And the guy sitting next to us snoring…" Melli started laughing, "That was hilarious!" She said. Everyone started laughing except for J. "I don't think that was funny at all," He said irritated. "Very annoying in fact." "Oh J, you're so serious…" He just looked at her sternly, as if his mind was made up and wasn't bending on his stance. "Are you for real?" She said, lowering her eyes to meet his, he held an airtight expression on his face. "Of course I am, the guy was like a canker sore for an hour, just snoring his brains out." "Lighten up." She replied, a little steam came off her forehead. "Oh, what the hell…" Sara said. "Are you almost there?" Sara asked the cab driver. "A few blocks." He replied.

Getting back to the hotel, Beau and his girlfriend left saying they would meet up another time, after J insisted they stay. They sensed J and Melli had something to work out, giving off an awkward vibe. Not the kind of confidence needed for a foursome, by any stretch of the imagination.

After a somewhat mediocre round of sex—at least compared to what they usually had— J and Mellodia shook themselves off of each other, no intimacy, just plugging away in their own worlds. Melli jumped into the shower, J would have to wait, and then she spent a good amount of time blow-drying her hair. "Are you almost done?" J pleaded. "You can use the shower if you want, if you need to so bad." "Yea, whatever, I've been waiting for nearly an hour!" "Why? Do you need to wash my scent off you?" "No. I feel like taking a shower, what is wrong with you?" He replied.

"What's wrong with me? What's wrong with you? You're about to throw a fit..." He ignored her getting undressed, he looked at himself in the mirror, the person looking back was a tired and miserable person. "How come you are always like this? You always get so serious and break the mood." "You're still talking?" J shouted. His angry voice escaped the bathroom. He jumped out at her as she was in front of a mirror teasing her hair still. "What the hell has gotten into you?" "Get out of my face." She said. "I'm not in your face. You're in my face with all your lip service. What's gotten into you?" She just looked at him like he was helpless, "Just look at you, you're so serious. You do this every time we go out in public, I can't believe you." "What? You're talking about that bum who was snoring, how I didn't think that was funny?" She scoffed, "You always have some excuse J..." He couldn't believe her argument, he stared her down, "Why are you focused on the small stuff? I took you out to dinner, we had a good time before that... We went to see the opera at the Met, what more do you want?" She looked at him struck by his passionate defense. "You're going to chastise me over something so small as that? It's over, no big deal..." He said. "It's always something J, you need to lighten up. It was funny." He shook his head, walked back into the shower. "It's not funny," He said, and then he turned the shower on, with the water drowning out his voice he said, "It's not goddamned funny."

In the shower, J recounted all the times Mellodia got down on him for petty things like this. It made him mad that she would be so ignorant and petty with their going out. 'I take her out, pay for everything, we go have a nice time, and she's stuck on this?' He thought to himself. 'Of all the things, she could focus on, it's about a small thing, about something that has nothing to do with us, where we're from, what we're doing in life... what are we doing?' J was getting ready to propose to her and her attitude towards him with Beau and Sara didn't seem like she was ready at all.

All the sex washed off J's body as he jumped out of the shower squeaky clean from the hotel-supplied shampoo and soap. The two of them were like magnets in bed, repelling each other, it was one tug after another for the sheets. Mellodia won that tug of war, as they fell asleep in the wee hours, J half-naked in his boxers.

The next day, J woke up from out of his spell, Mellodia was already getting ready, the two of them were entirely disenchanted by now. "Where are you going dressed like that?" J asked. "I'm going to see Sara, they invited me for brunch. "When? It's 9:30 in the morning..." "I texted them." She replied. "Well, I'll go with you..." "It's too late. I'm off now." She brushed up the rest of her eye make-up and gathered her purse; J was still stuck to the bed. "Give me a call if you have to." She said, then she ran to the door and left.

J just blinked irregularly, he couldn't believe what was going on, he was losing his girlfriend, he was losing the girl. He was losing his dream, and he couldn't take it anymore. The sex tape, the diamond ring, the petty dating faux pas'… this was supposed to lead to an engagement, not a breakup.

After the fifth attempt to call Mellodia' s phone, J finally left a message. He had become desperate, but also worried and tormented by the thought of spending the day alone in the hotel.

This seemed like cruel and unusual punishment, especially since they were on a couples' retreat. That night Mellodia returned to the hotel, J was drunk; the remnants of room service he had ordered were scattered all around the room, empty bottles were everywhere. Mellodia just laid herself to bed like nothing had happened at all, but things were not the same, something changed between them as a couple, they didn't know how to work through even the slightest errors in dating and company. The two of them were two damaged sex fiends, it's like they no longer needed each other, but Mellodia had the advantage. She knew J was more in love with her than she was with him.

Although they had great sex, Melli had to confront him with his rituals; she told him what she really thought. Truthfully, it creeped her out. They were so serious with each other, yet they were still scratching the surface of getting to know each other deeply. She felt he might have a couple unpleasant surprises. 'Maybe he really is some BDSM freak, or has some god-awful religious belief', she thought. At any rate, he could offer a strong backbone to rely on for her lifestyle to become a high-flying music professional.

By the time they made it to L.A. they were pretty much through. No matter how hard J tried to lay the honeymoon business on Mellodia, she just refused him. She reminded him how much he had lost his charm, his drunken antics were becoming wild and outrageous. His crazy sex rituals were just compulsions and scary nonsense to her. When they spoke, all she would do is nag about how they never had any fun going out, she left him dejected, even though they were supposed to be together. They just showed up together at industry events, when they needed something from one another.

It was no surprise that she would eventually leave him like a bad habit. The ring remained stowed away, without any proposal.

Mellodia decided she was going to forget about her past life, she would forget about "No-One-And-Done," Jimmy, Billy and J. She decided she would stay in Los Angeles. She had made all the contacts she needed and would pursue a job at a major studio. She did, and it was in a short amount of time. On the other hand, J was struggling for his life in L.A. He really shouldn't have stayed, but wasn't going to let go, he was going to stall his life back home if he could. Living off his savings, J stayed in Los Angeles, living in motels, pinching pennies wherever he could. He was stuck with Stockholm syndrome.

Mellodia began to experience morning sickness. She would toss and turn in the morning hours, blaming it on the food she ate from eating out, she drank very little alcohol, so it couldn't have been that. But it persisted. It worried her, to the point where she had to go to the doctor's. The doctor very confidently told her that she might have gotten pregnant, based on the symptoms.

"How could I be pregnant?" She asked. She hadn't had sex for a long while now. But after doing the math, there still was the possibility. The doctor recommended taking a pregnancy test, after doing so, the results came up positive, she was indeed pregnant.

It was like she had lost her mind, lost her job and lost her life in a single reading of the test. She tried a second time—a different method this time—still, the results came up positive. There was no use, 'I have to get an abortion', she thought.

She never said anything to J. But she could only hold out for so long; she was in fact pregnant now, and so she called him with the important news. Easing into the conversation she learned how he was now living in obscurity, not too far away from her. J had been stalking behind, living a penniless lifestyle in hopes of reaching his dreams with her and his career. His dreams were coming true he kept saying, the second she asked how he was doing, he was like a broken record though. She didn't want to hear it, but he thought if he kept her on the phone long enough he'd have a chance. So, when she told him she was pregnant, most likely with their child, instead of being distraught, he was secretly elated inside.

Her face braced itself solemnly to break the news to J, "I want to get an abortion," she told him over the phone. "You can't get an abortion Melli. No way. This is a life we're talking about." "You don't even know if the baby's yours." She replied. "What do you mean? Of course, it's mine." "So, what if I have this kid, then what? We're not living together, we're not married. We're not even together…" She sulked.

"What if we got married?" He replied in earnest. Mellodia' s heart went into the pit of her stomach. She was shocked and horrified. 'Who was J really?' She wasn't ready for all this reality to settle in, a wave of trepidation crept into her skin. Marriage equaled death to her. Although she found J warm and charming at times, she couldn't conceal how through she was with him. "I've been living poor, pinching pennies, hustling my ass off with interviews, I'm confident I'll get a good job here, soon. Plus, I have a lot saved up, if I sell everything back home, we'd be able to live well… think about it Mel." "What the hell are you talking about?" She asked furiously. "And, since when do you call me Mel? We don't work together. We don't work, period." "Why don't you understand?" He asked earnestly. "I have a fucking plan Melli, you think I'm just a poor beggar? I'm working for us. I know what you want, and I know what I want. We're going to make it. I know it." She didn't seem moved by his testimony, but she also didn't contest his argument.

Being bound to someone like J left many questions unanswered, but her scared emotions burned off as soon as she surmised his wealth, if, in fact he was going to do what he said he would do. She would be able to live securely to pursue her travels and make a name for herself in the music business a lot easier with financial support. And single life had been dragging her down.

It was clear to J, Mellodia seemed somewhat distressed. He took a deep breath and smiled at her infectiously, "You remember when we first met…? On the boulevard?" She finally exhaled, letting her tensions go. "Ya," she answered. "It wasn't that long ago you know…" He said. She couldn't help but smile. "How did we know we were going to see each other again?" She shook her head. He continued, "I would have died if I couldn't be with you Melli. From the first time, I met you, it's like we knew each other already. I fell in love with you at first sight. This is meant to be, Melli, we're meant to be." He said. She was taken by his passion, feeling mixed emotions, it was influencing her to all the positives about what they had. She started thinking more about what she would be leaving behind, and her prospects didn't look half as promising. Although J was a loveable creature, and seductive at times, she didn't have the same kind of passion for him as he had for her. He was still more in love with her.

Unsure of how she was going to deal with this whole predicament, she retreated for a couple days to her parent's house for the weekend, to break the heavy news. J insisted he meet with her family, but she refused, wanting time for herself. She went alone.

110

At her parent's house, she was reminded of how far she had come, with her career, her lifestyle, all her accomplishments and ambitions. Something told her she would have a better life with J, but she didn't want to admit it, because it would be settling, something she never wanted to do.

The house was like a still photograph, in a very quaint and settled country atmosphere. Family portraits lined the wall, black & white, sepia, and some color photos. Mellodia couldn't stop thinking what family life would be like. "Do you know if it's a girl or a boy?" Her mother asked. "I'm having an abortion." She replied abruptly. "Oh no! Melli you can't do that! You have to have this baby. Plus, you said that your boyfriend has intentions on keeping honest, he does sound like a very fine man. You said you loved him…" "That was then. This is now. I want my life. Once I have a child, that's all gone." He mother breathed in deeply. "Your father and I agree, we want to see you succeed in your career, but your boyfriends have all been less than perfect, sweetheart. From what you're saying about J, it sounds like he's more of a reliable person, and that he's serious. You can rely on a man when he has it all together. And we're more than happy to take care of your baby when you need us to." Mellodia began to cry, overwhelmed by emotion. "You'll be fine, Mellodia, oh it's alright…it's alright, oh, don't cry…"

At the doctor's, she asked his advice about the abortion, if she could have a chance at her life still. "It's your choice." The doctor said. "You can decide whether you want to have this baby." He assured her. "If I choose to have an abortion, won't the baby feel pain?" She asked. "You have until the end of next month, it's still just a fetus." She wasn't convinced. He made it sound like it was removing a mole.

◊ ◊ ◊ ◊

Mellodia eventually went through with the abortion. When she returned to L.A., it was a done deal. She went against her family's and J's wishes, but she wanted her independence, it gave her a clean break to make it in the music business.

Luckily, J landed an important job in marketing for a major book publisher, He was back, in a sense. but his social life was waning. Racing up and down the wide and empty streets in his sports car wasn't the same as Limerick Boulevard, he didn't enjoy the chase like he did when he was back home, it was more of a drag. Dating was a lot easier with friends; and, of course, a lot easier on the Boulevard. The irony was, J and Mellodia ended up in the same city, but separated. Both were single and the arts were their life, but they may as well could have been living on distant planets.

111

It was too easy for her to say no to his half-baked marriage proposal over the phone. He didn't even know where she lived, he just called her on the phone. It was sad really. He tried to guess where Melli would be. Lost in an oasis, there were way too many streets to narrow it down, but he knew the vicinity of where she lived. Every chance he got, he raced up and down the main street near her house, there were all kinds of people, all very jaunt and busy city people. Some ugly, some pretty, short, tall, fat, diminutive, clownish, serious; there were always new faces, every day.

Thousands of people separated him from Melli, but he wasn't going down without a fight, if only he could find out which apartment building she lived in. Neither was he going to call her anymore, out of fear that he might scare her away completely. He nearly lost all hope until one evening he spotted her on her way home near the block that he had been circling for weeks. It drove him crazy, there she was, his life right in front of him, five miles from where he lived, and thousands of miles away from where they came from.

J had an airplane write out in the sky a couple days later lettering the words, "I heart Melli". She had seen it, but never dreamed it was for her. There were plenty of Melli's in Los Angeles. But she couldn't deny when the words "I heart Mellodia" were written in the sky.

When he thought of a more intimate way to touch her, J became anxious. He was starting to lose patience; he didn't want to lose it all. At least he knew the vicinity of where she would be, so he hired a troubadour. He paid them handsomely to strut up and down the boulevard playing songs to serenade everyone, and eventually Melli. He instructed them to travel up and down the block where J had spotted Mellodia on her way home from the grocery store. They were given a description and picture of her and the time of day she would most likely be out. It was a long shot, but J was losing hope.

They were able to spot her for a moment, they played the song J instructed them to play, the one he wrote for her.

"Hey girl you know that you're one in my heart, right from the very start…"

She found it charming, but somehow didn't make the connection still, this was J orchestrating the entire thing. The next time J accompanied the troubadour, around the time they said they had previously spotted her. She would most likely be strolling on her way to her apartment. After a couple songs and strumming down the block they spotted her. It was Mellodia at last! When she noticed J she became so excited she could hardly speak.

He approached her, singing his heart out to her. They looked at each other, all the tears in their eyes were dry, they couldn't cry.

J was near his mission. He got down on one knee and proposed to her on the spot, while the emotions were sky high. The lucky devil that he was… he got her to say 'yes'! She didn't even know what his living situation was, if it was better or worse than before, she was swept away, it was clear that they were truly meant to be in this one moment's time. He had done this all for her, and was still crazy about her.

They re-united in a hug, for the first time in a long time. J picked her up in his arms and carried her away, driving off in the sunset, this time on a new boulevard.

◊ ◊ ◊ ◊

The Phantom's Comeback

I'm a dark person with a few nasty scares, and a lot to hide, so I made sure the theater was dark when I appeared on stage for the premiering of my movie. I was dressed in nearly all black, wearing a tight blazer. A mask awkwardly bulged out of my vest pocket, the nose was too large to neatly tuck away, it just looked like I had more muscles than I did. The mask is not one of a clown's, but a jack-of-all-trade's. And tonight, was a full house. I would show and tell for an interview at the theater, so that later I would be paid.

All I could see were a pair of a thousand eyes focusing on me as I walked on stage. A huge round of applause… What for? I have no idea, because none of these people knew who I was, or at least what I was about, at least not yet… I shook the interviewer's hand and quickly sat down in my highchair. I made sure there would be no lights on me.

The interviewer grabbed the mic and spoke loud and clear, "Ladies and gentlemen, it's my pleasure today to introduce to you our guest, young Edo, in this true-life segment about his late friend, Arsenio, this movie recounts their come-uppance around a string of well-known parties. Known simply as young Edo, he is with us today to shed some light on the subject. Isn't that right?" The interviewer grinned devilishly as he turned for a split-second, "Young Edo everybody!" The audience roared in cheers, I felt hot, all at once, I jumped up out of my seat, somewhat compulsively; I took a bow and got back in my seat as soon as I could. "Tell us your story, and this documentary we're about to watch."

He waited for me to take the floor. I hesitated, looking at him maybe a fraction of a second too long. He gave me a snotty look, one of a wimp. He also came across fake, his words and demeanor were one of someone who didn't know story at all. He certainly didn't know who I was, or about where I was from. He was scared to even look me in the eye, but I wasn't here to entertain him, I was here to entertain the thousands of people in the audience. I breathed in deeply…

"The movie is my personal testimony, my side of the story, if you will, of a time that captured the attention of a lot of people during our so-called 'List' parties. These parties brought us to light before anyone ever knew me—or Arsenio—or knew that we were the orchestrators of these parties. The stories were one of scandal, love, envy, run-ins with the police, run-ins with neighbors, fights, drugs, games, celebrity, politicians, famous athletes, musicians… you name it, and they had come.

These parties were an underground phenomenon, and Arsenio was the orchestrator of the whole thing. Not too many people knew who he was behind the mask. That's how it all got started really, the masks… Wearing the masks was not only an infatuation, it was an addiction. There was a mask for each day of the week, at one point. They were the sort of masks that put all other masks to shame; a twist on the classic Commedia Dell'Arte masks, you know? Some were beautiful, some comical, but most were ugly, dark and twisted. Like this one…" I pulled out the mask, it was a black, sinister looking one with the classic long-nose.

"Will you put it on, so everyone can see?" The spotlights went on. I shook my head furiously— 'no'. The interviewer cued the spotlights to turn away from me. I hadn't agreed to that. "Let's get a spotlight on just the mask then." He held it in the spotlight so everyone could see, I was merely a shadow next to it. "Really? Wow." He just examined it in horror. "Scary stuff! So, this was Arsenio's favorite? What made him so crazy for masks?" He asked.

"I think how unaccepting people were of him." I replied, "People said he stared… or that he was weird, or that he was sad, or gay. He was the subject of sociopaths. The mask didn't make him look good, or any better, in fact. It was a crutch. But like any addict would tell you, that's what makes an addict who he is…"

114

— "I see. I see… So, Edo, what would you say is the message of this doc?"

— "The message…?"

— "Yeah, or the message you were getting across with your lifestyles?"

— "No message… it's about love, in an unforgiving world, the sweetness, the despair. The lust for a woman in a dark and twisted universe. you will learn fairly quickly, though… love conquers all. Is that a message?"

— "No, well, I guess not…"

A silent pause, there was nothing left to say. The director took his cue to cut the lights as the air had been sucked out of the theater, and the movie began, a fade-in and voiceover began narrating on-screen…

◊ ◊ ◊ ◊

'…I once felt love, I once was alive, brimming with excitement for all the lovely coquettes, fair ladies, merry wives; and, of course, the fine goddesses themselves, the precious young women of society. I wrote to them, called to them and sung beautiful notes that only a young man could sing before his fall. I learned early on from my protégée, Arsenio… once you had one, you had them all. It was so true. Yet, they were so irresistible, flocking at what was our entourage at the time. I suppose I misunderstood the true meaning of what he had meant. You only have one true love, you see? But once you have it, you can have it all; I got greedy. I wanted them all. If not for myself, then just for the sake of staking a claim in other women's hearts.

Arsenio is dead now, I live on a small boat parked in the harbor next to where I first met him. It wasn't long ago that we were playing charades at sea, conquering the world. Sometimes, I take the boat for a sail to reminisce of the glory days. My life has changed, ultimately for the worse. I hit rock bottom, like a dead cat, never quite able to spring back to life.

I'm looked down upon, I'm seen as a leper, an inconnu, a mere shadow…

'You see my scar?' The camera focused away from my protruding face as I jutted it out. He waved it off and said, 'Yes I can see it… go ahead, please tell your story…'

115

— 'Where was I?'

— 'Rock bottom…'

'Oh ya…' The camera angle focused on me again, the director now taking a drag of a cigarette, sitting in his high chair.

'…It wasn't long ago that I was revered. It's hard to imagine now, but I was a quiet force, and yes, I was adored by women. I don't have a fraction of the wealth and popularity that I had then, but I still manage to get by. I've dreamt of moving back to Italy countless times, where I'm from, but I don't have enough money, you know, to live the way I want to live… I get lucky occasionally, but only from those women who know my story; and even then, they are with me out of pity. I'm only left with memories, and a haunting nightmare of what left me the way I am today. Arsenio's death was said to be unsolved, a few people said that he had survived, that he was still alive. But I saw it happen, all of it. I assure you, he died. Arsenio is dead…

It was the night of midnight mass, I was driving with Arsenio in the passenger seat. A car had pulled up from the right of us and opened fire. It wasn't a random act of violence. The shooter was attempting to steal a briefcase of money that we had just made way with from an extraordinary stunt we had pulled at a producer's villa. It was a couple minutes before midnight, and we got shot at a red light, 6 blocks away from the church. He died instantly from a gunshot wound to the head."

"I'm sorry…"

"It's okay. That's all ancient history now…"

◊ ◊ ◊ ◊

'How did you and Arsenio meet?'

'I first met Arsenio on his yacht, before any of the infamous masked parties, thanks to my best friend at the time, Horace. He introduced me to all his entourage. They were a fun crowd, but some people I felt had issues… eiher with personal relationships, or in their lives, in general. They were TV and film stars, workaholics, fanatics, epicureans, and a few everyday people, a couple of your run-of-the-mill work, all of them with a bad habit of partying too much.

If it wasn't for my friend Horace, I wouldn't have become involved with them, and wouldn't have come to know Arsenio. At the time, Arsenio was looking to make an impression on his yacht, it was on loan, he had sold a stake in his family business, a string of small, local theaters.

I'll never forget how we were with me, Horace, and Angelica—Horace's girlfriend at the time. She had been an actress in Italy from our home town of Florence. She was a living, breathing, specimen of beauty. Also, remarkably loud and obnoxious, she would say curious things, though she was quite intelligent, she was just how I imagined a cinema star to be. The day we met, we were directed to pull a stunt of cinematic proportions, to make the scene, really. I agreed to it. After, we would kick off an intoxicating amount of legendary parties, it was the equivalent of overnight fame, masks.

He already had a handsome mask for me, I tried it on and fell in love. It was a thrill ride. Since, Arsenio had belonged to the football legends of Florence, he had been given a nickname. His true name remains unknown to me… but he was thought to be related to Pedro II, the last emperor of Brazil, which meant he spoke Italian with a distinct accent and spoke fluent Portuguese. He spoke English too, but with a heavy accent, just as I did.

"You don't have an accent now…"

"Yes, well, thank you… I have improved it dramatically throughout the years."

"You said Arsenio was a football or soccer star?"

'Soccer, forgive me, that's what I meant to say, not quite a star, but a very much a player. Frankly, he was a weird personality, overly proper, strangely flighty on and off the field. His manners were too mild for sports, not aggressive enough. Yet, he was exuberant, the minute he could start moving his hands in conversation. He played soccer well, but it was his persona that made him a legend.'

"How about you? You played too, didn't you?"

'Of course. Of course I played…'

'I was known as Edo, my birthname's Edson, like the great Pélé. I also scored the most goals with a bicycle kick in the Serie 'A', which gave me bragging rights in la liga. After my short-lived career, I was later known as young Edo, which was for my personality as a playboy. I built up a decent reputation for being a playboy, in fact. That's how I met Horace. We met during a model runway show. I was there to visit one of my crushes at the time, while Horace was there to take pictures and shoot videos non-stop with the models and other recognizable people. I made no reservations about who I was, and what I was there to do. People were charmed right away by the confidence we possessed.

It wasn't like I was there to court the girls or get married, or that I was making friends with the girl for the first time. Of course, I had an eye on her. I was crazy about her, and all women like her, she wasn't just a model, she was a model for all women I liked. We consumed each other and everyone else around us at the show, she was like an abyss, with a bright, white complexion. She wasn't white, she was a mixed white, an exotic, beautiful thing of a bird, everything I wanted. I hate to admit it, but that was all I really wanted at the time. It ended up becoming a one-night stand, basically. Seeing us talk must have been like watching a cityscape from a telescope for my friend. There's something completely lost in translation when viewing lovers from outside. They don't understand the mania, the passion, and all the nonsense, what it means. It wasn't conversation, but engagement, a proposition into what can only be sex, romance and lust. It was a story of two people pursuing sex, either one folds, or the other one convinces the other it's not about sex, but both are seducers, and both are seduced. To us, love was a battlefield, we waged war and claimed victories in the most outlandish ways.

Horace occupied himself by taking pictures and making movies. He had been attempting to find his muse, when deep down he knew she was in fact a young woman who he had met in passing at one of the runway shoots, so he continued to make his videos and take his pictures. He worshipped her, somehow, in his thoughts, but never spoke to her directly. A 25-year-old woman... I'm not sure who fell harder, him or me...

That same day I met the model was the day I met Arsenio for the first time, on the yacht. We started on a ferry on our way to a Mediterranean island. The other woman I met on the boat was a beautiful, blonde-haired American. I could tell she was American right away, the way she smiled, that look of charm, innocence and familiarity, yet not a stranger to sin.

She was a vision to say the least, a woman who made the world easily perceivable, she was like god in the flesh, highly impressive, like tall American

118

women I had met. Before I could even ask Arsenio who or what she was, she had mounted a platform to speak in front of everyone on the boat about something I knew nothing about, to save endangered animals apparently.

Her speech was short and sweet, afterwards, she was swept with a frenzy of picture taking and chatter. Of course, when the ferry stopped, it was no mind to anyone, the captain distracted everyone to one side of the boat. 'Dolphins! Look!' Someone shouted, before I could follow the crowd, Horace yanked me by the arm and had me follow him and his entourage down a narrow stairwell on the other side of the boat.

There stood a brand-new speedboat, small and inconspicuous, with a serious looking man driving it. He couldn't help but light up with one look at the beautiful blonde. We quickly jumped on and were escorted away watching the crowd on the ferry behind us. They became smaller and smaller as we distanced ourselves from them. It felt like we were going 200 miles an hour bouncing through the sea at these speeds.

The beautiful blonde right in front of me, the laconic feeling of being at sea, the salt from the water misting in front of us, it was all very much a moment for me. As I looked back I could see the ferry rapidly disappearing, it was still stopped for the dolphin watching.

It was the first time I had experienced a trapdoor at sea, this was all new to me. Although, I didn't know who the blonde was, it was like meeting for the first time in a long time.

It wasn't long until we climbed out of the speedboat, just south of where the ferry was heading… and mounted the gold-lettered yacht that was on loan. It had all the luxuries and amenities only available to the super wealthy. We could see the ferry slowly making its way to the harbor as we luxuriated on this rich yacht. Truthfully, we got bored to death. Trying to make conversation, the woman couldn't stop messing with her hair, and chatting about how she wanted a pet tiger, but her neighbors wouldn't allow it—or, how the city ruled against drinking outside. It took me a while to understand what she was saying, I just kept watching her lips move the whole time, making out bits and pieces.

We were all lying in wait, feeling like we needed something to do… anything… But we kept it cool, I still was on a high from the whole experience, anyways. We slowly trickled along the bay. The ferry we had jumped off of was

119

finally reaching shore. The people had no choice but to see us. It was all done in true Italian fashion, if you ask me, showing off in front of a populated shoreline. People had no choice but to see this spectacle, like the breaching of a blue whale, our yacht slowly glided and commanded the attention of a sizable audience. 'How is it possible?' People whispered. 'Les Dauphins.' Someone said in French. Of course, the crowd couldn't believe it, we were like a dream, a hallucination to them. A diamond encrusted necklace seemed to shine even brighter on the beautiful. She had a glowing tan that made her look very Mediterranean, and gorgeous, candy-colored yes. relate to. And then the enigma, Arsenio, who posed like a show dog.

That night was our debut, Arsenio gained instant recognition on the island, we had started one of what would be countless parties. As for our relationship, he became my mentor; I, his protégé. But my story doesn't begin there, no… It starts in the old world of Italy, where I was born. My story is about a struggling youth who became a playboy.

◊ ◊ ◊ ◊

'In the old-world people took their time. We lived our life in anticipation— waiting, for friends, waiting for food, for anything good really… waiting for the local grocer for treats, waiting for family and friends, or for the teacher to bend over and cross her legs. Anything worthwhile takes time. They say time is money, but some things are priceless.

I moved to New York as an adult. It was a whole new scene, a whole new everything to me. Everyone was rude to me, they said I asked too many questions, I was constantly waiting for a reply, totally confused by their abruptness. People thought I was stupid because I spoke so slow. Their expressions were also a lot different. I couldn't understand the expression, 'If you can make it here, you can make it anywhere.' I used to think, 'so if you can make it anywhere, why do you make it here?' I didn't understand. It took me a little while to make it on my own, but I learned very quickly. I didn't amount to much in the eyes of blue-blooded Americans, most of them well above my level of education and ranking in society as far as money was concerned. They were bourgeois, rude and overly confident, very cocky, but they didn't show off. We were weird animals to them. But I had gained a good amount of respect among Italian-Americans. And there were a lot, most were involved in the rubbish and restaurant businesses, many had family-run businesses; restaurants and various food stands. They were not the same restaurants I was used to, everyone here wanted their food pronto. Everything was done pronto. In the old world, things were done much more carefully.

The first time I stepped onto the streets, I was bombarded with police sirens and ambulances. People dying from drug overdoses, suicide, or murder. It took me a long time to get used to, those types of things rarely happened in the old world; and, if it ever did, it was kept hush-hush. If someone died like that, it was kept a mystery, under wraps. The deceased always had an accident, nothing was ever intentional.

This new mentality was also very hostile. Most of the Italians here knew very little Italian, maybe a few dozen words, but no more. And they would repeat themselves constantly. The fact that I was born and bred in Italy and not a total F.O.B. gave me credibility in some way, but made me less a person in another way. They would point to me and repeat what I had said, they would ask me to translate and speak to their friends and relatives who spoke Italian. They had no idea I was South American blood, that that was the main reason for coming to America, because amongst certain Italians, I wasn't even considered Italian. I was dropped from a racist football club in the 'Serie A'. It was a version of Jim Crow, except if you had a drop of any blood other than Sicilian or Italian, you were not considered Italian, at all.

◊ ◊ ◊ ◊

Growing up, I always had an insatiable appetite for women, there were a few women I adored who inspired that sense of female worship. One of my aunt's friends especially, a truly precocious woman, would cradle me, and love me like a doll. She nurtured a love inside me that would grow until I became an adult. I learned to appreciate a woman's gestures at a young age, the mannerisms of such a lady was delicate, always with a pleasing look on her face, but that look would change to detestation any time someone spoke coarsely with her. My boyish charm and sun-bright complexion made her so happy to see me, especially since I was one of a few young boys in her life. This appreciation for women lasted until my teenage years, when I was forced to work to make a life for myself.

I had tried everything from working at local grocery stores, pawn shops and even the overnight shift at the local ports, but none of these jobs had lasted very long. I finally gave in and put in my calling card at a nearby talent agency, essentially a modeling agency for tall guys and a hiring spot for specialty escorts—a specialty escort was an unspoken agreement for those who had talent but not quite model material. I fell into this category. At the time, I hadn't had enough experience in life to fulfill the role of any kind of real escort, I was still a teenager, basically. All my experiences were with other infatuated teenage girls, nothing that was worthy of payment. Although I was out of luck with this ambitious endeavor, I was fortunate enough to have met a local shoe-shop owner who I had met going to-and-fro' the agency. He had one of the finest shoe stores in town—or, anywhere for that matter. His name was a very long, distinguished one, but most people called him by his nickname, Freddo. People would come from all over just to make a purchase there. Freddo was well known, very strapping and a cunning shoe salesman, Freddo was one to move and shake with Europe's elite.

I knew him only in passing, I admired his ways and his store very much. He knew who I was as a budding football player. He liked football, a lot, and supported our youth club. Best of all, he liked me. On few occasions, I checked to see if he was in, on my way to the agency. He wasn't at the shoe store often, but he wasn't hard to spot. He drove a bright, yellow Bugatti parked out front...

Sometimes, he would make a special trip either to meet with a rich customer, or for a meeting with his employees. But he gave off a scent, and it was a bold one. It had been meeting with somebody, on one of the days I was passing by his store. I noticed his Bugatti had been recently detailed. I peered in to see who was there, it was a very charming, young woman, trying on heels. She was the daughter of one of Europe's most powerful diplomats, barely the age of majority, and she was buying nearly half the store. I slowed down walking past the store, and waited for her to leave the store. She was carrying an awkward number of bags. I whistled to her, to get her attention, offering to help, but she insisted she would make it to her car by herself.

She was parked up the street on a somewhat steep hill, as I recall. I could tell Freddo had been flustered, he didn't dare insist because of her being so young. As she stepped on the sidewalk, I caught a look of hope, almost panic in Freddo's eye, as if forcing me to help her carry her bags. Before he could open his mouth, I volunteered myself and ran across the street, helping the young girl without any resistance from her now, I offered to carry most of her bags and walk her to her car up the steep street.

'What's your name?' I eventually asked.

I tried breaking the silence. She just flung her long ponytail to the side.

'Angelica...' She said.

I didn't know what to say, I could have walked and carried her bags all day, but with nothing to say at that point. I wanted to ask her a few more questions, but she already was acting like I was of interest to her. 'You don't talk?' 'Me?' I replied. 'Sure, I talk. Why, what do you want to talk about?' I could have bit my tongue off, I lost my mind. Every time she looked me in the eye, I fell into a dream. I recognized who she was—a heiress, very sweet looking and beautiful—but I was nobody, I never would have dreamed that this girl would want to talk to me. We stopped at a red light before crossing, I tried not to look, but couldn't help myself.

'My car is a couple blocks up.' She said. When we crossed, I very quickly brushed ahead of her to stay on her curbside. It was an act of chivalry that I took somewhat seriously. Typically, men were supposed to walk nearest the road when walking alongside a lady. I had switched the bags to my left hand now as we walked up the inclined street. She looked at me very quickly, like she wanted to say something, but she got the picture. I worked for a living, she was an heiress, I really had nothing to say to her. We walked up one more block to her tiny Fiat, a car barely able to fit two people. I carefully packed all the bags as it filled the entire passenger seat, I even swiftly got the door for her as she clambered into the car on the driver side. Still without any resistance from her, she gave me the sweetest, brightest smile. 'That's it.' I thought. Now she's gone, no tip. That's okay, I was able to meet her, at least.' I automatically turned away, darting back down the street, but before I could leave... 'Wait a minute!' She yelped. She drove up in her car, and flicked out her wrist, fanning large-faced bills at me. 'You didn't think I was going to leave you like that, did you?' I chuckled, gay as can be. I was very much surprised. 'Thank you!' I said, somewhat surprised. 'Do you work at the shoe store? Do you work for Freddo?' She asked. 'No.' I said. 'I don't.' She gave me another look, 'I'll put in the good word for you, next time I'm there. Well, whenever I'm in Firenze at least. What's your name?' 'Edo.' I said. She looked at me and told me she liked me. My face must have lit up again, I didn't know what to say all over again. The words, 'I like you too', spilled out of my mouth. She giggled, waving me goodbye, her hair frayed out the window as she sped away in her tiny car.

It wasn't much long after that I began working as a shoe salesman. There I learned to appreciate the beauty of a woman in an intense, yet distant way. I was meant to upkeep the store most of the time; that included sweeping floors, double-checking the orders and accounting, cleaning the windows, making sure the store window looked good; and, from time-to-time, I would sell shoes. Given this was a store for women, it took a great deal of care and patience to be able to deal with the whim of a woman holding a credit card. They were a heart full of emotions at the sight of high heels.

123

The store supplied the finest shoes, mostly hand-made ones, a few from Morocco, a few from other countries, but mostly made in Italy. When there wasn't a list of guests, or Freddo's personal clients, I was given the responsibility of fitting. Under the supervision of a mentor, I was eventually able to ring up my own sales and work as a full-commission salesperson. That was essentially the pinnacle of this career, but I learned so much more when I had been a mere associate tending the store and fitting shoes. I stayed so busy as an associate that I had become accustomed to rarely looking at the customer while fitting. I was a blind lover of women's feet. I learned how to perfectly fit a pair of high-heels, and how to size up fit and style for each pair of feet. I learned the art and practice of perfect fitting. If I looked, she would become emotional and wouldn't buy, she would prefer a more expensive pair, or one that was a more commercial look, but not the one for her. So, I kept my head down and stayed busy, making small talk when I had to. I got so good and instinctive that I could make small talk without her even thinking twice about which pair she was trying on. I learned a lot about women, a whole lot. There was an invisible field between them and myself, the walls came down, and my instinctive abilities were enhanced, my mind was freed of all the ideas that once trapped my thinking of how I believed a woman was, and what they needed. I found out what women truly wanted, and learned some of their secrets.

◊ ◊ ◊ ◊

It was around the time I had been promoted there that I received a call for a gig, I had been working towards. I remember it well, it was exciting, a turning point in my life. I paid my dues, and now I was going to get lucky again. The call was from the lead female agent, she was very excitable and spoke loudly on the phone, it sounded like she was nearly out of breath. 'I need someone who can stand. Can you do that?' She asked. 'Yes…' 'Perfect!' She shouted. 'I saw your headshot, you're exactly what we need, you can stand for a long time?' 'Yes, of course.' 'Yes…? One other thing Edo, and it's a big one… how tan are you, are you still tan?' She asked. I couldn't understand the question. I'm a dark-complexioned person, perhaps more so than the average Italian, but I still thought it was a trick question. 'What do you mean? That's my skin color. I was born this way.' 'Beautiful!' She smooched me a kiss, 'You're available both nights, yes?' I told her yes, of course I was, I had worked and waited for the past year and a half for one of her gigs. She smooched kisses over the phone again, and then hung up.

The gig was for a museum, I was made to be an Egyptian god, the first time my South American blood gave me a break as an Italian, it was very ironic. The agency didn't have a big mix of different talent. All the other models were either too pale or too dark. But, it was lucky for me because I fit the role perfectly, and it made my debut.

Unlike other models, I spent the entire week working as much as I could, because I knew I would need the rest before that weekend. The other models were somewhat lazy and very pretentious. They hung around cafes mocking people, or being bastards at bars, restaurants and salons. They felt entitled to everything, never feeling the need to work for their job, or to improve. Most of them were taller than me, but honestly, based on their attitude, they didn't have anything to back it up. They talked a good game, to make up for what they lacked in talent.

That weekend at the museum I was fully prepared. I had made sure to get a lot of rest the day before the other models were wrecked from too much drinking, and sleep deprivation.

Honestly, standing in one place for 5 or 6 hours seemed kind of silly to me, and easy, but it was a little more demanding than I thought. The whole time we were meant to look the part, that meant keeping our bodies and faces contorted in the same position, and we had to stay clean and dry from all the sweat. Modeling was something new to me, but performing wasn't. I had many years competing under my belt, I knew how important it was to prepare myself for this weekend. After our first work break, standing five hours in front of the museum, the other models were wasted, they began complaining of every little thing, plus they looked like shit.

As the evening progressed I was getting more and more attention while the other models were panting like dogs. Eventually, I was given the role for the museum. I would get oiled up, stripped down to my bare skin, half naked, and adorned in gold and Egyptian regalia. The agency insisted on putting make-up on me, but I refused. I had never worn make-up and wasn't making any exceptions. I became a weekend fixture around the museum, like an animated statue. I became familiar, and was rarely found out of character. It was very exciting at times. It was like winning an Olympic medal every weekend.

I was instructed not to talk to the passers-by, but I did anyway, not very much, but sometimes. The people liked me, they would nod, say hello to me, some even tipped me, but there were also critics. Naysayers would look at me and comment how gratuitous I was, just standing there as a model, a piece of wasted talent. It made me somewhat self-conscious. After all, I was working to be an escort, not a statue, and high-end escorts needed to be confident, and have know-how. It wasn't until I had met a couple the last weekend of the summer that I knew I could be a successful escort, just based on the talent I already had. They were a middle-aged couple, the man's wife was very emotional, she was having an episode, pushing him away from her. Before they even passed by me I could feel her looking right at me. When she got close enough, she made sure to let me know that she liked what she saw by the way she was checking me out. They ordered a coffee and sat down right next to where I was standing. The man was calm and collected, being very confident, despite his wife's arguments. 'You don't love me.' She said. 'You don't let me love you.' He said. 'You're seeing other women, I know it.' She shouted. 'Now stop, stop!' He said. They kept quarreling like this for nearly half an hour, it felt like a very long time, anyhow. She continued searching for attention, in need of outside affection, locking her eyes on me. I must admit, she was sexy, and impressed, but it didn't move me. I continued to contort my face and stay in character. Having a job helped with my confidence. A younger me would have jumped at the opportunity to take advantage of the situation. As their stay progressed she became more and more emotional, and needy, begging for attention. She had my attention, the crowd had thinned down, and they were as much a spectacle as me now, what else was there to look at? They passed by me, she was tugging on her husband's sleeve like a child in need of candy. 'What?! He hollered. Then she looked at me, not able to make her plea. I smiled, she was cute, after all. Their voices were fading away. A few people still were exiting the museum near closing time. It was always refreshing to see the crowd leaving the museum. They were a lot more joyful, and full of great ideas, versus the patrons entering. Those people entering the museum were always in a mad rush, and mean. The people exiting smiled and were pleasant, like a breath of fresh air.

It was 10:30, and I was about ready to call it a night. I probably could have stood there for another 8-hour shift. I was confident of my work performance, but not of my future as a model or escort. A fig tree next to where I was standing began to shake viciously. I was startled for a moment, branches, leaves and figs fell to the ground. At first I thought it was an earthquake, then I heard that angry woman's husband squeamishly shouting, he was hanging off a branch. I looked up, I saw his shadow, he managed to get himself tangled up so bad that he was forced to jump to the ground from nearly 15 feet up. A tumble roll cushioned his fall, he even twirled around after landing with figs in hand half-comedic, as if he were a gymnast. It was an impressive spectacle, almost miraculous for someone as chubby as he was. The angry wife stared at him for a long moment, 'You're crazy!' She yelled.

— 'Here, have a fig.' He handed her the fruit. I remember it very vividly now… 'You want one?' He asked me, bringing them to my face like they were a pair

126

of balls, he lowered them to show me. I knew what he was doing. He was trying to influence me, and I could tell he was very persuasive, but I was still in character. He was not at all satisfied with my lack of response. A smug look, 'What's your name?' He asked. 'Edo', I replied. 'Edo! Like Edson—?' 'Yes.' 'Edilson?' 'Like Edson.' When I got a close look of him, he was very familiar to me, I had seen him before, but now it looked like he was wearing about twenty pounds too much. He tapped my shoulder, and pulled me underneath the brightest light. Seeing me there he was reminded of the situation. Before I could say or ask anything, his wife chimed in. 'Look at him. He's perfect!' She said. 'Hey, easy, I'm still right here, you know? You look so familiar', he said to me. 'You played football?' I nodded, 'yes'. I didn't want to give too much away, I was still at work, after all. 'You did play football, yes?' 'Yes.' I replied. 'What club?' 'Firenze.' 'Ah, that's right, okay, yes I know who you are now…' And then the wife approached me, still not looking, she asked her husband, 'Can I touch him?' He gave her a careful look, 'Touch?' 'Yes, I want to feel him, touch him, to make sure he's real.' He put his hands on me, brushing my arm, 'It's okay, yes?' I smiled, still in character. She looked at me with her desperate eyes, her nails were too long, her skin was tightened from cosmetic product and plastic surgery. She was very beautiful, but looked a little worn. She began to lightly graze my forearm. I involuntarily squinted a little. 'Oh-ho-oh..!' The husband belted out a great, big laugh. 'He doesn't like it. A-ha-ha!' She looked down somewhat bashful and then she looked at me again, like she wanted to eat me up. I smiled, and then she grabbed my bare arm, squeezed my muscles, and started to pet harder. Now I was getting a workout. 'Mmmm' She moaned. Her husband turned away, he wasn't looking at this point. She gave my lower body a good check-up. I must say, it was very arousing. A couple passers-by witnessed this frisky pat down, they snickered and mocked from a distance, and she became tamed again, ashamed of her lust. She tried petting me lightly once more. I didn't like it. I flicked her away, and finally she stopped. 'He's so perfect. Isn't he?' 'What? You want to take him home?' She just looked at me a little lost. 'Look, you see? He doesn't want it…' He winked at me. 'You see, you have to be with me. I'm the one for you, don't you see? Because I love you…' It seemed she was giving in. He brought the two figs that looked like a nut-sack to her mouth. 'Eat.' She took a big sensual bite; without biting down, she looked at me again, fig in mouth. I could have worked deep into the night after this encounter. 'C'mon, let's go now.' He insisted. She shook her head. 'No! I want it with him…' 'What? You serious? What did we just talk about?' His mood changed, he looked to me for my support, but when he noticed I wasn't objecting to the proposition he seemed somewhat defeated. He looked at her, looked at me another time, up and down, carefully studying, then he looked at her, carefully, for a second time. She was beaming a smile, gaily in the light. It was clear. She won her battle. 'Okay…' He said, finally. He jiggled his keychain out of his pocket and threw them at me in the air, they were keys to an exotic. 'Can you drive…?' He snickered, 'It's okay, yes?' Without waiting for a reply, he walked his wife to the car. I followed. That was the start to my years as a high-end escort.'

◊ ◊ ◊ ◊

— 'Wow, that really is sensational. What about the actual movie? Tell me more about the night of the movie deal that led to the tragic end… what happened that night?'

—'Okay, yeah…well, what started as a double-down bet on a movie reel pick-up ended Arsenio's life. The movie, as everyone will see, was—or is—a sensational telling of what made us little-known socialites with the so-called 'List' parties.

The name for it started as one of my official bookings while I was working as an escort. It was basically one big affair. There was a guest list, of course, but there was also a host list, basically, of famous people. And then an auction held to pick the 'Who's Who' for a dinner date with a lucky guest. Everyone has a list, you know what I mean? Anyone they would want to be with despite their vows, or standing relationship.

Now that I think of it, I'm surprised it didn't come about sooner, people would speak about their so-called list, and it would grow so much that I wasn't sure if these people even cared about being in a real relationship. Needless to say, this became one popular party. A lot of emotions were at stake, and a lot of money. People forked over thousands of dollars to be in a lottery running to be with a celebrity of their dreams—sometimes even husbands forked over money, just to pacify their wife's crazed obsessions. But everyone had a fantasy, and it was trendy.

My job was to host and serve tables. Some of our very own were there, it was a jackpot night for us. For those who didn't want to go through with it, or couldn't afford the auction, or "have dinner," they could always sock away their fears and dismay by going out with one of us. It was a consolation prize, included in the gratuity, if you will.

When we had these large parties, we brought up the idea to these famous people, and a lot of people were game. Arsenio and I basically re-worked the concept and turned it into a live firework show, so to speak…

And it wasn't as loud and obnoxious as your usual house party. It was more on an engagement for a couple's party. Some were formal, some were casual, all were approaching a climax, a fulfillment of a dream; a bold, extra-marital affair. I wasn't a lackey escort in a bow-tie anymore, this had become a legitimate business for us. We raised hundreds of thousands of dollars for a single dinner engagement at times.

◊ ◊ ◊ ◊

—'What about the movie deal? Can you talk more about that?'

—'Yes, of course…first, we were told this movie would only get sold for a fair price, if Arsenio delivered the reel in person, and only if he played a game of Russian roulette at the party. That was the setup. He had agreed, it was nothing new to him. The agent said there was nothing to worry about, it was simply one of their fancies…for personal entertainment. What the producers never realized was Arsenio played Russian roulette in his sleep, and had grown up in and around circuses since birth. Naturally, he took the challenge, perhaps more boldly than he should have.

So, he arrives at the villa with the reel, mind you, the place reeked of sex and crushed spirits. It was a very sad place. I was holding the reel in my hands. We were in desperate need of cash and had just reached the rock bottom, so we thought…

Before knocking on the door, someone let us in, no introduction, no salutation, nothing. We entered. Resting right before us was a huge black suitcase, as was promised, in exchange for the movie. The one you're about to watch. It was set up like a prop, everything about the producer's villa looked and felt like a booby trap. We could hear the faint sound of conversation in the living room, through the narrow kitchen hallway, the entire house was very dark. We walked in blind, having to push through shadows and empty space in this make-believe house. Stepping into the kitchen—the producer, Antoine, stepped toward us, a flask in hand, greeting us in the most intimidating way possible. I admit, my heart skipped a beat, I was startled. 'Glass of wine?' He asked. He poured a glass and led us into the living room.

It was French 57'ish in the room, a dark and austere room, which included an opulent bar. A room of people darted their eyes around me like voyeurs who were only seeking a peep show, and nothing more. 'Arsenio, I want you to meet Lane, he's one of the executives.' The man was almost ashamed, like maybe he shouldn't have been introduced. What I liked about the producer was how bold and daring he was. That resonated with me, that was the kind of personality it took to deal with Arsenio.

129

The vibe at the villa was very tense, like a time bomb was about to go off; one intense moment after another.

We were in front of everyone like a staged Mexican standoff, there was nothing left to do but watch. Delicately putting on gloves, the producer unsheathed a revolver and winked at me. He handled it very carefully in front of everyone, like it was a diamond necklace or something. Opening the chamber, he placed a single bullet inside and gave it a loud spin. Before handing it off, he quickly put the gun back in his coat, and pulled it back out, along with an elastic velvet glove. He handed it over and said, 'Just in case it turns into a CSI scene here.' One of the executives gave out a bold chuckle at this. Smiling wide, Arsenio delicately received the gun, telling him, 'That's okay. I've never been afraid of making a scene. I trust you.' 'Touché!' The producer cried. Lane just gulped and watched as Arsenio put the gun and glove in his own coat, and pulled the gun back out by itself. This, of course, was not the same revolver, it was his own with a trick safety on it. It was a magic trick he had been perfecting for years, the gun would only fire if the trigger was pulled a certain way, so the trick was to pull the trigger as though it didn't have a safety on it. Sure enough, he aimed it at his own head, delicately, patiently, and waited for a dramatic pause. He closed his eyes and fired. 'Click', the gun made the same sound as though it had an empty chamber. There was no response. Like a compulsive maniac Arsenio spun the revolver once more, rapidly pointed the gun to his head and pulled the trigger once more. 'Click'. This time he fell to the floor, comically pretending to have just shot himself.

Still thinking the magic was his own, the producer clapped and everybody began to laugh at the fake death. 'Bravo, bravo…' He said. We sat with them. They were all swigging their glasses, still very silent, like vipers. There was a long pause, until he asked, 'Why'd you do it?' The producer asked. Arsenio just stared him down, undeterred.

— 'What? Why'd I do what?' Arsenio asked.

— 'Why'd you bite the bullet?'

— 'Why'd I bite the bullet? What do you mean… figuratively?'

He got emotional, 'Yeah sure, figuratively!' He said, 'You just pointed a gun at your face and pulled the trigger… why?'

A huge smile came across Arsenio's face. Motioning for the producer to hand him the gun. The producer hesitated, and reluctantly gave it back to him, saying, 'You're not going to shoot yourself for real now, are you?'

— 'I'm already dead…'

He opened the revolver to show, it was fully loaded. 'You see?' Everybody's jaws dropped. The producer had a moment of curiosity, as if to ask how the hell he pulled it off. Everybody lit up with big grins. It was what they needed, a darker magic.

— 'So, do we have a deal?'

— 'Anything.' He replied.

The movie abruptly ended with a smash cut to a black screen.

"So, I asked for the final cut for the movie in addition to the movie." The final credits rolled including the following text:

SOME ANIMALS WERE HARMED IN THE MAKING OF THIS MOVIE...

BASED ON A TRUE STORY,

TO BE RELEASED…

A long pause exhausted the theater's attention for a moment, the interview was in shock too, the room was just still silence until Edo started to casually speak on stage.

—"The music was of course mine too. I never told anyone that." The lights went back on, with a spot on Edo and the interviewer.

—"What does it mean that YOU asked for the final cut?"

— "I am Arsenio…"

I then put on the mask. Hopefully, no one saw my hideous scars in plain sight.

— "You're Arsenio? How? I thought Arsenio was dead!"

— "I was born Edson Dobini III. My nickname was Edo growing up in Florence. My parents abandoned me for the circus at a very young age. They were circus people… I never learned of them, but I recognize them when I'm there, at carnivals… Everything in this movie is true, except for my death, and the telling of the character Edo, that was simply me of course, and a few other things…"

— "What about the autopsy? And, how is it that people think you're dead?"

— "The gunshot wound, it was very severe, as you can see... I had been officially dead for a short period of time, in a coma, before miraculously coming back to life… I suppose God knew my true intention the night of midnight mass before being shot."

— "So how is it no one found out you were in fact not dead?!"

— "I requested the doctor to proclaim me deceased, if anyone outside were to ask. But, it was easy to keep under wraps. I am no one famous, I am no one special. I have no more than a few records to my name, no family, only a few friends… just like my parents, I am the mask that I wear."

Before saying another word, I jumped out of my seat and bolted off stage to quickly exit the theater. Many would request the favor after that night's showing, but I answered to no one. I'm busy perfecting another illusion… the mask shouldn't fool anyone now, it's how I deal…

◊ ◊ ◊ ◊